THE NIGHT THE MISTLETOE DIED

A MODERN CHRISTMAS FAIRYTALE

S J CRABB

Copyright © S J Crabb 2024
V17112024
S J Crabb has asserted her rights under the Copyright, Designs and Patents Act 1988 to be identified as the Author of this work.

This book is a work of fiction and except in the case of historical fact, any resemblance to actual persons, living or dead, is purely coincidental.
All rights reserved. No part of this book may be reproduced or transmitted in any form without written permission of the author, except by a reviewer who may quote brief passages for review purposes only.

NB: This book uses UK spelling.

WHY I WROTE THIS BOOK

Granthaven is based on a real place and this story is loosely based on that.

I changed the name, but it is a magical place that went up for sale as a whole this year. All of the houses, farms and buildings, including the lake, manor house and church, were included and if I had in excess of thirty million pounds, I wouldn't hesitate to buy it.

I wondered who would.

Would it become a business or remain in private ownership?

It sparked my imagination though, and I couldn't wait to write a fictitious story about it.

We now live in a different world and reality is taking over our lives online and on television. We are fascinated by other people's lives and idolise celebrity. I'm no different. I am fascinated too and the two celebrities in my story - although fictitious - are living the impossible dream.

Real life merges with the fabricated one in my story

and reveals the most interesting things are the cracks. We are all humans doing the best we can and shouldn't compare ourselves to people who appear to be living the life we want for ourselves.

Maybe that life doesn't really exist.

I loved writing this story and hope you enjoy reading it.

Whether you are reading it at Christmas or sometime in between, may I wish you a happy and healthy life and a very Merry Christmas.

Sharon xx

THE NIGHT THE MISTLETOE DIED

A fun and festive Christmas delight.

When the famous footballer Luke Adams inherits a remote village, he arrives with his influencer girlfriend and a reality TV crew, ready to document the happy occasion. But all the villagers want is for him to restore their village to its former glory.

Luke and his girlfriend are shocked by the village's rundown state. With the condition that he can't sell the inheritance for a year, Luke resigns himself to wait it out, counting down the days until he can return to his privileged life.

Then he meets Jessy Potter, a captivating local whose warmth and loyalty to the village make him question everything. She's unlike anyone he's met, and soon he's drawn to her in a way he didn't expect.

As Christmas approaches, Luke is cast opposite Jessy in the village play and sparks fly between them, despite their efforts to resist. But with the village's future hanging in the balance, and his current relationship complicating things, Luke faces a choice that will change everything.

Can he bring the village back to life—and find a way to bridge the gap between his world and Jessy's, or will his famous relationship stand in the way, and the scandal recorded for prime-time viewing on Christmas Day?

For fans of all things Christmas, this heartwarming romance takes you on a festive journey, where life's biggest

decisions are made under the glow of holiday lights. A sweet, charming, opposites-attract love story with no cheating!
 Perfect for the holiday season.

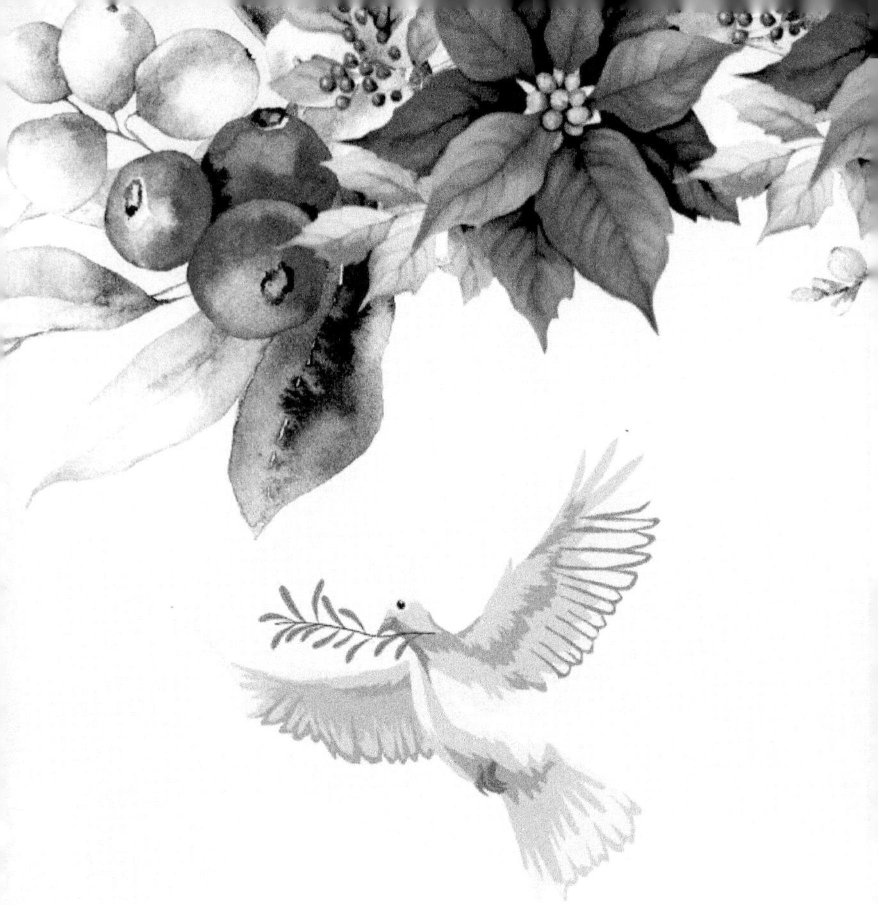

PROLOGUE
LUKE

Manchester – England

When fifty-three thousand people fall silent, it's as if time stands still. As I lie on my back, staring up at the concerned faces peering down at me, it's as if I'm one of those patient observers.

It doesn't even hurt. Ricky's expression tells me I should be worried – but I'm not. If anything, I'm numb to it.

The coach shakes his head and nods to the team, who signals for a stretcher. My ankle throbs but the adrenalin is acting as a heavy dose of pain relief.

I don't even consider the implications of my fall. I twisted my ankle – big deal. I probably tore a hamstring in the process. It will heal.

Coach shakes his head and whispers in my ear, "There's nothing to worry about, Luke. We'll take care of it."

His expression tells a different story, but the pain is now firmly in charge and as the medics head onto the field, the silence from the crowd is more deafening than their cries.

It's as if this moment changes my life. I'm not sure why. As I'm lifted onto the stretcher and carried from the field, the noise from the crowd is unleashed and serenades my exit from the field of dreams into an uncertain future and oddly the only emotion I'm experiencing now is relief.

~

FOR IMMEDIATE RELEASE
Luke Adams Sidelined Due to Injury

Manchester, England — November 23rd, 2024 — Manchester Rangers regretfully announce that their star footballer Luke Adams has sustained an injury that will sideline him for an indefinite period. Initial assessments suggest a broken ankle and torn hamstring.

Adams has been instrumental in the team's success this season, scoring ten goals and five assists. His absence will undoubtedly be felt by teammates, coaches, and fans alike.

Team medical staff are currently working closely with Adams to determine the full extent of the injury and to develop a comprehensive recovery plan. Head Coach Donahue expressed confidence in Adams' resilience and commitment to returning stronger than ever.

"Luke is a fighter and an integral part of our team," said Coach Donahue. "While this is a challenging time for him and the entire squad, we are optimistic about his recovery and look forward to seeing him back on the field."

The Rangers appreciate the ongoing support from fans and the broader community during this time. Further updates on Adams' condition and expected return will be provided as more information becomes available.

For more information, please contact:

Sandy Barnes

Press officer

∽

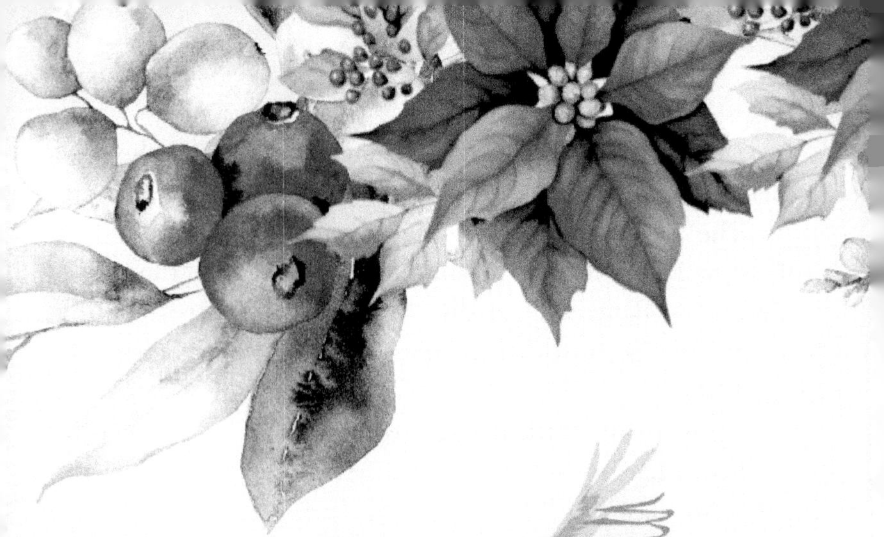

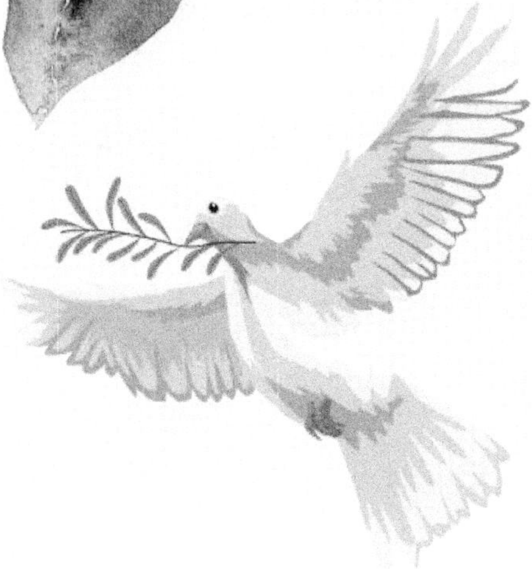

CHAPTER 1
JESSY

It's so cold. Freezing, in fact, and I pull my padded coat around me as tightly as possible as I gingerly make my way across the frozen cobbles.

It wouldn't be so bad if the place I'm heading to was warm, but heating is a luxury the village hall can't afford and I resign myself to blue fingers and toes by the end of the next arduous hour.

As I push open the huge wooden oak door, my friend Angie offers me a similar frozen smile that is edged in despair and a yearning to be anywhere else but here.

As I take the seat beside her, she whispers, "Have you heard the news?"

I roll my eyes. "Yes, I've heard the news and, to be honest, that's all we need."

I smile at the spark of excitement in her eyes because Angie is a sucker for gossip and entertainment news, and I knew she would be beside herself at the headlines this morning.

. . .

Injured premier league footballer Luke Adams to convalesce at Grantley Manor.

Yes, that's all we need when our village is facing the biggest crisis in its history because one woman died exactly one month ago.

Lady Christabel Townsend. The woman who owned Grantley Manor and everything in the vicinity, finally took her last breath and plunged the village into uncertainty.

She left behind a two thousand acre estate with an impressive Grade II Listed family home and the entire village, including all its properties, to her heir.

In its entirety.

It's the entirety that concerns the village because where Chrissie was a much loved landlady who was most definitely one of us, it's uncertain if the new owner will be as easygoing.

I note the strained smiles of my neighbours as they whisper in small groups.

The estate owns all of our homes, thirty-two of them, all on short-term rentals, as well as the local church, this village hall and the surrounding countryside, including several derelict barns and a working farm.

The manor house has ten bedrooms, which causes concern at the prospect of a hotel chain buying up the lot and bringing strangers to Granthaven.

It's why Mr Spalding, the head of the resident's committee, called this meeting and as my parents are on a mini break to Vienna, I am the unfortunate idiot here in their place.

The man himself clears his throat, and the steam from his breath warms the frozen air as he shivers against the cold.

"I called this meeting to order to discuss the sad passing of our valued friend and landlady, Lady Townsend."

There are a few murmurs from the depleted gathering because it appears that most of the residents are Christmas shopping in nearby Dorchester, or tucked up in their decrepit cottages watching a Christmas movie while they shiver under their duvets.

For all her kindness, Lady Townsend was a terrible businesswoman, and the estate has fallen into a stare of disrepair that some would call poverty.

It's only because we loved her so much that nobody made a fuss and just pulled together to help one another as the properties fell deeper into ruin.

The manor house was just another victim, and I'm terrified that the new owner will sell it off to big business, who will erase our way of life with their bulldozers and start everything anew.

As crisis committees go, this one has no power and I'm aware any rights we had died with Lady Townsend.

As expected, we spend the next sixty minutes going around in circles as we attempt to patch another hole in our sinking ship. At the end of it, the conclusion is to go ahead with the village pantomime and try to have a bloody good Christmas and see what the new year brings.

As we attempt to file out of the village hall, it's painful to walk and Angie links her arm in mine and whispers,

"Come to mine. The fire's going and mum's making mince pies."

"Thanks."

I smile gratefully because my house is freezing, due to the fact my parents forgot to order the logs and there are only so many damp twigs the wood burner can cope with. There is no central heating – that packed up and left years ago and the hot water is limited to one bath a day, which is not enough to warm my legs, let alone sink into it and wallow in decadence.

Angie's cottage is almost luxurious as we push through the door and her mum greets us with a cheery, "How did it go?"

Angie rolls her eyes because her parents never involve themselves in village meetings and have always sent their nosy daughter instead.

"Usual." Angie grumbles, and I take a seat beside her, enjoying the warmth of the fire as it melts away my misery.

Margery hands me a steaming mug of tea and smiles sympathetically. "You can stay here if you want, Jess. Your house must be an igloo by now."

"Thanks."

I smile gratefully as I take a sip of the hot, sweet drink and wish my parents were half as domesticated as Margery Barnes. She is the mother in the ads. Loving and sweet with an endless supply of freshly baked delights and unwavering gossip. She is fun too and staying here will be a relief because I spend most of my time here, anyway.

Sir Barkalot jumps onto my lap and I'm grateful for

his warm furry body adding another layer of heat as I feed him the crumbs from a home made biscuit that Margery placed on the table beside me.

Angie sighs dreamily. "I can't believe it. A proper star is coming to town this Christmas and I'm more excited than if Christ rose again and joined in the birthday celebrations."

Margery shakes her head. "I wouldn't be impressed by a footballer, love. Guys like that aren't like us. They live in mansions and drive Ferraris and have model girlfriends. He will take one look at Grantley Manor and jump back into his sports car and head to the nearest tropical island for Christmas. Don't get your hopes up."

Angie shrugs as she wraps two hands around the warm mug.

"He arrives tomorrow, apparently."

"How do you know?" I'm curious as to where Angie gets her information, and she winks slyly.

"Karen Sims. She was told to prepare the Manor House for ten people."

"Ten!"

I stare at her in shock. Karen is the ageing housekeeper that kept Lady Townsend company more than she did any work, and I'm guessing she's grumbling about the fact she must actually do some work for a change.

Margery nods. "I heard that too. She's asked for volunteers to help ready the house for the visitors."

Angie's eyes light up and she stares at me with excitement.

"We should so do that. It will be a chance to take a good look around and possibly even get a thank you from the man himself. What do you say? Are you up for it, Jess?"

The sad fact is, I have nothing better to do this weekend, so with a sigh, I squeeze Mr Barkalot and smile. "Sure. Why not?"

CHAPTER 2
LUKE

Morgana is excited. Just the spark in her eyes and the way her chest falls and rises rapidly causes my heart to sink.

"This is amazing, Luke. I can't believe it."

She taps her perfectly manicured fingernails against her phone that I'm almost certain is permanently glued to her hand.

"Just think about the opportunities your injury has given us. It's the gift that will keep on giving."

I stare at the cast on my foot and say sarcastically, "I'm glad to be of service."

Her eyes shine. "Oh, this is pure gold. A manor house in the English countryside – at Christmas no less. Just imagine the pictures."

I shake my head and reach for the glass of brandy that is fast becoming my new best friend.

"If you say so."

"Oh, but I do, Luke. Imagine it. Roaring fires and candlelight. The scent of mulled wine and crisp pinecones hanging heavy in the air. A beautiful tree with the fairy lights flickering against a backdrop of elegance."

She says dreamily, "We will be dressed in Christmas sweaters and bobble hats. Imagine the wholesome scene as we gaze fondly into one another's eyes as the locals serenade us with carols around the huge tree."

I tune out because once Morgana gets going, we could well be here for some time.

However, this time, I don't have the luxury of oblivion as the producer interjects.

"It may work. What about an engagement ring cleverly disguised in wrapping under the tree, facilitating a romantic proposal on Christmas Eve? It will precede a fairy tale ending when you receive the news that you're back in training in the new year, leaving Morgana to plan the wedding of the century."

"Perfect."

Morgana claps her hands together. "I would host – sorry, babe – *we* would host a huge Christmas themed engagement party. I'll use 'Events Are Us' as they've been reliable in the past."

I glance at my agent, Steven, who is currently playing a game on his phone and I wonder if I'm the only sane person in the room right now.

The brandy burns a trail down my throat as I note the score at halftime, wishing like crazy I was there to help the guys out.

But I won't be.

Not for the next three months, at least, while my injury heals and the subsequent physio determines whether I'll ever play again.

Morgana carries on with her excited chatter. "We

were so lucky your aunt died now when we most needed the exposure."

I raise my eyes and even Steven pauses mid-stream.

Morgana shrugs. "I mean, obviously we're sad. Nobody wants anyone to actually die but now she has, it couldn't have been better timed. That's all I'm saying."

The director adds, "What Morgana means is it's a gift we should unwrap before Christmas. This is the perfect opportunity to cash in on your problems."

He starts to pace the room and flings his arms around with excitement.

"I'm seeing Christmas renovation."

His voice rises. "You head home to your crumbling ruin."

Morgana raises her eyes. "Wait, what?"

He interrupts. "It will be like something out of a Dickens movie. The villagers will be so grateful that a star has descended among them. They will look on you as their saviour as you begin to piece together their broken lives and we will be there, recording the moment for posterity. Interviewing the grateful peasants and glorifying in the renovation as you breathe new life into the place that time forgot."

He clasps his hands together and squeals. "I'm seeing a romantic proposal. Down on one knee."

I groan as I shift my cast bound leg and he says quickly, "Obviously when your cast is off. How long until that happens?"

Steven adds, "Two weeks."

"Perfect."

Jasper grins. "We have exactly four weeks to make this happen. It will require some editing in the new year, possibly working through Christmas and it may take a Christmas miracle to achieve it all, but with everyone's agreement we can make this work."

All eyes are fixed on me as they wait for the green light and I drain the brandy from the glass and note another goal scored against us from the image on my phone.

Morgana is staring at me with hope-filled eyes, and even Steven is motionless as they wait for my acceptance of the situation.

My thoughts turn to my Aunt Christabel. A distant relative that we never visited. I believe my father fell out with her years ago and subsequently they never reconciled before she died. That is possibly why she left him out of her will and gifted me the albatross that hung around her neck and I can't even sell the bloody carcass because the will states I must live there for one year before selling.

I close my eyes as the tension increases in the room and I know everyone's hopes are placed firmly in my direction. They are relying on me. The villagers in Granthaven are relying on me and all I want is another shot of brandy to drown my misery before I watch the football highlights.

"Whatever." I shrug and Morgana squeals with triumph and fist bumps Jasper as they fall into a huddle where words such as 'followers' and 'ratings' emerge from their excited conversation. Steven merely grunts and returns to his game, and I turn my attention to drowning my sorrows once again.

CHAPTER 3
JESSY

If I was cold in the village hall, it was positively tropical compared to this place.

Angie glances around in dismay at the crumbling walls and floors with holes in them. The furniture is old, although Karen describes it as antique, and her positivity is the only good thing about this place.

"I never realised it was so–" Angie shrugs. "Decrepit."

I nod, shivering as an icy gust from the nearby sash window creeps around my soul like an icy gloved hand.

It's the kind of place you want to wipe your feet on the way out and I shake my head sadly. "Poor Lady Townsend. I'm surprised she lasted as long as she did in this igloo."

Karen bustles into the room with a heap of linen. I would say fresh, but from the yellow tinge, I would surmise it's been relocated from the attic trunk.

"She never lived in these rooms. She had two rooms that are adequately heated and more than enough for her."

She thrusts the linen at Angie and groans, peering around the room with an expression of defeat before the challenge has even started.

"There are ten bedrooms spread over three floors. I suggest we start on the first floor and work our way up. Valerie and I will begin on the left-hand side of the staircase while you can start on the right."

"What do we have to do?" Angie says in dismay, and Karen shrugs.

"Try to make it habitable, I'm guessing. Make up the beds, clean the dust and the bathrooms. I'll hoover through when we're ready and Bert is gathering whatever passes as floral decoration from the garden in an attempt to brighten the place up."

"When is *he* coming?"

Angie asks the only important question and Karen groans. "Tomorrow, can you believe."

She ticks off the names with her fingers. "Luke Adams, of course, and his girlfriend, Morgana."

"Wow!" Angie's eyes widen. "You know, she has five million followers on Instagram, and I watch all her vlogs. I can't believe she is coming to Granthaven. I'm so excited."

Karen doesn't look quite so impressed and huffs, "I wouldn't know anything about that. Anyway, they are bringing a film crew with them to record a fly on the wall reality series about their move to the country and the inheritance. They will be filming throughout the Christmas period and I can do with this like a hole in Santa's sack as he flies around the country."

"Well, I can't wait."

Angie's eyes are shining with excitement, but I share

Karen's dismay. She is right. This is the last thing this village needs. Some arrogant, spoilt premier league footballer, with more money than sense and his vapid girlfriend with fake hair and nails and a fake life, probably. I hate them both already.

I'm already regretting volunteering at all, but the chance to peer inside Granthaven Manor was an opportunity too good to pass up and as we climb the grand staircase, I can sense the history creaking in the walls and under every footstep I make.

We find ourselves in one of the bedrooms and Angie gazes around in awe at the faded chintz and threadbare rugs on the floorboards.

"I bet this was so grand back in the day." She says reverently, and I must agree. The entire house has been neglected and allowed to fall into ruin and all because one family fell apart and the owner no longer had the ability to maintain it.

I wander across to one of the floor to ceiling windows that gazes out on the vast grounds, at the end of which is the pride and joy of the village – the huge lake.

Angie groans and says over her shoulder, "I'll take the room next door. Good luck with the dust."

As she leaves me alone, I stare out of the window and a sparkle of sunshine touches the window pane. It's as if I am transported back in time as I gaze out on a scene that has probably never changed. It's as if time has no consequence and I picture the many people who have also enjoyed this view and wonder about their lives.

If anything, I am incredibly sad as I realise how far this house has fallen and reluctantly, I tear my gaze away from the view and set about making the space liveable again.

There are five bedrooms on the first floor, along with one dressing room adjacent to the master suite and four bathrooms. There is also an ironing room, a staff sitting room and a lift to move between floors without coping with the stairs.

Somehow, we manage to make them barely liveable and Karen appears satisfied as she inspects our handiwork.

"Bert will light the fires in every room the morning before they arrive. It's a lot to do and I doubt the guests will know how to work the wood burners, but they'll have to learn fast if they don't want to freeze."

Karen rolls her eyes. "I give them one night before they're heading back to their pampered lives and forgetting this place even exists before they place it up for sale and pocket the proceeds."

"I heard they can't." Valerie interrupts. "Mr Spalding told my Bert that the footballer who inherited it all must live here for one year before he can list it for sale."

She laughs. "It will be fun to watch him slum it with the rest of us and who knows, we may even score some repairs out of him before he sells up."

I gaze at her thoughtfully, because this is right up my street.

Business.

I have just finished a business degree at university and am waiting to hear back from several interviews I have attended since graduating. I'm hoping to move to London, or at least an actual city because my shelf life here has long since expired. As a child, it was the perfect place to live, but as a young woman with hopes and dreams, it's the last place I want to be.

Yes, the suggestions I could make regarding this place would be many, and yet I doubt I'll even meet the new owner, let alone offer him the benefit of my freshly learned wisdom.

CHAPTER 4
LUKE

My first view of Granthaven Manor and the village as a whole is from the air. Rather than face the horrific road journey that would take several hours, Jasper hired a helicopter to fly us here from Manchester. The film crew are taking the arduous road journey and subsequently we arrive way before them.

"Wow, Luke, this place is amazing!" Morgana cries out, as we glimpse at the beautiful landscape and quaint stone cottages with thatched roofs.

"I'm so excited!" She squeals, the noise echoing inside my headset and I run my finger around it, edging it away from my ear drum.

I know she's excited. This is the gift she's been waiting for. A reality TV show and endless photo opportunities. She is champing at the bit, ready to take the internet by storm, and I smile when I note her outfit, chosen especially for the occasion.

She is wearing suede black leggings with a white silk

shirt, over which is an aviator jacket with a Burberry scarf tied around her neck. Her long blonde hair is curled and styled to perfection and she is wearing a fur bandana around her head. Her bright red painted lips are stretched in a blazing smile and her porcelain veneers sparkle against the sunlight. She is clutching her Chanel bag, her Cartier watch gleaming on her wrist, her feet encased in UGG boots.

Morgana is and always will be a designer's dream.

She is laden with exquisite jewellery and has taken many selfies and photos of us both in the helicopter that she has subsequently edited on the flight and posted to her Instagram story. She has also filmed various parts of the journey as she shares our move to the back of beyond.

I peer with interest at Granthaven Manor as we circle overhead and note the proud stone walls and the extensive grounds surrounding it. "It's huge!" Morgana squeals and grips my arm with excitement and Steven turns from his seat in front and rolls his eyes. It makes me chuckle softly as she snaps more photographs and then says loudly, "When we land, I need a few shots with Luke as we exit the helicopter. Jasper–" She turns to the producer. "Is the photographer waiting?"

"Only a local one, I'm afraid, but his work checks out and he has assured me of his professionalism."

"Good."

Morgana nods as if satisfied, and as the helicopter touches down, she turns to me and smiles. "This is it, Luke. We have arrived."

"So it would seem."

Despite how much I hate all of this, I don't hate her and note she's like a kid on Christmas day as she falls into her element. I've learned to let her work while I observe and merely pose for the shots she needs when asked to ensure a harmonious environment.

Personally, if I had my way, I would never pose for another photograph in my life. This is what I hate about my profession. The endless press calls and photos. Sponsor commitments, modelling the latest fashion item or the latest brand of aftershave. Expensive cars, watches and exotic holidays all come with the job, as well as the newly built mansion in Cheshire, equipped with a gym and cinema room as standard, not to mention the indoor and outdoor pools.

This life is generous, but it wants its pound of flesh and as Morgana said, we have been gifted an opportunity, but I'm guessing mine is completely different to hers.

It gives me breathing space. A well-earned rest if you like, and I could certainly do without this inheritance right now. From what I know of the property, it comes with a load of baggage that I am ill-equipped to bear and yet I'll have to step up because it's mine to keep going for one more year.

I will definitely sell. Why wouldn't I? The agents have valued the entire estate at over thirty million pounds. It is more money than I ever dreamed of, even though I earn a hefty three million pounds in salary and a further three million from sponsorship deals and my share portfolio.

Thirty million though is life-changing and I would never have to kick a ball again. Then again, I no longer do it for the money, anyway. I do it because it defines me. Without football I have no purpose in life and it has been a part of me for so long now, I can't remember a time when I wasn't kicking a ball toward a net.

"Luke, darling, we need you."

Morgana's shrill voice permeates my nostalgia, and I turn and fix an indulgent smile on my face as I drop my arm around her shoulders, making sure to gaze into her eyes like a besotted fool.

"Perfect." The photographer says with a broad smile and nods toward the place I must now call home.

"What about one outside the front door as you prepare to go inside?"

Jasper nods enthusiastically. "Super, although we will re-shoot the scene when the film crew arrive but it's important to mark the occasion."

I stare up at the solid oak door and note the scratches and grooves of a life well spent. It's as if every line has a story to tell, and I can sense the history of the place as I gaze at it in awe.

Morgana slips her hand on my arm and says softly, "Don't worry, Luke. I'll appoint an interior designer asap. We'll drag this crumbling ruin into the modern age if it kills me."

She has a wistful expression on her face as she whispers, "I'm thinking modern traditional. A beautiful solid oak door with a huge brass knocker and definitely a wreath attached. Two huge bay trees will stand in pots on either side and a portico – yes, that would work."

She shakes herself out of her dream and smiles. "Leave it with me, honey. I'm a whizz at interior design."

I smile for the camera but resist rolling my eyes because Morgana obviously believes replacing like for like is a good use of my money. I prefer the door etched in secrets and mystery over a fabricated lookalike one with no history whatsoever.

Once again, my thoughts turn to my aunt and I am sad I never visited her here when she was alive.

It's taken her death to force me to visit, and I don't like how that makes me feel.

~

We head inside and a woman stands watching us with a wry smile.

"Welcome to Granthaven Manor, Mr Adams, Miss, um–"

"Morgana." She smiles brightly. "Just the one name. That's all I need."

The woman nods and says warmly, "I'm Karen Sims. Your aunt's housekeeper."

"Oh, poor Aunt Christabelle."

Morgana actually wipes a tear from her eye and says sadly, "I never even got to meet the darling. I imagine she was a magnificent example of humanity."

I step in quickly. "Anyway, thank you so much for looking after her. I am very grateful."

I sense Morgana tense a little beside me and notice the horror on her face as she gazes around the impressive entrance hall.

She shivers and wraps her arms around her body and says incredulously, "My goodness, it's like a freezer in here. Isn't the heating on?"

"There is no heating." Karen shrugs. "Unless you count the woodburners in every room. Bert has lit them all, so perhaps you will be more comfortable in the sitting room. It's smaller than the drawing room and heats up quicker."

"Fantastic! Show us the way."

Morgana offers another, slightly less radiant smile, and as we follow the formidable housekeeper, she whispers, "Goodness, Luke, shall I ask Steven to arrange a plumber? I can't survive without the central heating on."

I notice Steven pocketing his phone and call out, "Morgana wants central heating installed. What do you say, Steven?"

"I'll look into it." Is his gruff reply and I turn back to her with a soft smile. "There you go. Your wish is my command."

She nods happily and as we follow Karen, I laugh to myself. It's a trick that always works because Steven tries his best not to spend any money because he's as tight as a frozen tap, which is why I pretend he controls my finances, because it ensures I keep hold of them. I'm surprised Morgana hasn't worked that out yet, and it gives me somebody to blame when her wishes never happen. Yes, Steven is a valued member of my team and he earns a lot of money from me as a result.

We step inside the sitting room and Morgana's gasp echoes around it as I stare at a space that has been decorated in neglect. The faded upholstery on the sofa tells of a once grand piece of furniture, along with two wing-backed chairs set beside an open fire that is the only life in the room.

The chairs appear dusty and threadbare and their cushions are minus any stuffing, it seems.

The rugs are just about clinging onto life, but speak of the mystery of far-off lands where they began their lives.

An ancient coffee table rests nearby with several water marks stained into the grain, a layer of dust clinging to the cobwebs underneath, obviously overlooked as a cloth wiped the top layer away.

"Luke." Morgana is speechless and can only say my name as she stares at the once grand room. The windows, although impressive, are framed by faded curtains that disguise dirty glass that may not have been cleaned for years.

"This room smells funny."

Morgana screws up her nose and stares in horror at the threadbare chairs and Karen says kindly, "I admit it needs a fresh coat of paint and some updating, but it's been a happy home and I'm positive will be again."

Her cheery sentence is at odds with the view and my heart sinks as Morgana whispers, "I can't stay here."

"Nonsense dear." Karen steps toward her and smiles kindly. "You'll soon get used to it. It's what we call cosy. You'll love it in no time."

If anything, the room fills me with sadness because it merely demonstrates what happens when nobody cares anymore. I'm guessing this was once a vibrant room, full of life and splendour that has fallen into disrepair through lack of money and enthusiasm.

Steven says gruffly, "There's a hotel in Dorchester. They have three rooms available."

Morgana spins on her heels and smiles with relief. "Oh, goody. That sounds super."

She takes a deep breath and says calmly, "We will return tomorrow with an interior designer. What we need now is a nice hot bath, some amazing food and wine and a decent night's sleep."

She turns to the housekeeper. "Thank you so much, Karen. I appreciate all of your hard work in preparing this um–" She wrinkles her nose. "Um, amazing house, but we couldn't possibly stay here without central heating."

Karen shrugs. "The entire village is without central heating and we manage."

"Are you serious?"

Morgana's eyes widen and before she can insult the kind housekeeper any further, I say quickly, "Steven, take Morgana to the hotel, Jasper, too. I'll stay here and Karen can show me around."

"You're not joining us?" Morgana's eyes widen in disbelief and I smile softly. "No. I'll be okay. I could use the time alone, anyway. It's been a lot to take in, and I would appreciate the time to see what I've inherited."

"Well, if you're sure, hun."

Morgana steps towards me and kisses me on both cheeks and smiles sweetly. "Enjoy, and you know where we are if you change your mind. We'll be back in the morning."

I'm certain she breaks the record for exiting a room and Steven rolls his eyes as I mouth, "Thank you." Before he turns and ushers a horror-struck Jasper from the room. I'm guessing his four-week schedule is slightly longer now and out of everything that has happened so far, that has brought the brightest smile to my face.

As they leave and the house falls silent, I smile at Karen and say politely, "Please, can you show me around? I can't wait to see the rest of the house."

CHAPTER 5
JESSY

Angie sighs heavily. "Have you tried calling it?"

"How can I call my phone when that's what I lost?"

I stare around me in dismay, hating that I feel as if my right arm has been cut off.

"I hate being so dependent on a microchip." I grumble as I turf out the contents of my bag one more time, hoping I merely overlooked it before.

"I'll call it then."

Angie calls the number and we fall silent, straining to hear the familiar ringtone.

We are greeted by silence, causing my heart to sink. "Where could it be?"

I drop down into the chair by the warm fire and gaze at my friend with despair.

"You must have left it at Granthaven Manor." She says with a rueful smile.

"Possibly."

I wrack my brains to picture where I had it last and

sigh when I remember I left it on the side of the bathroom vanity unit when I used the facilities.

"I'll have to go back there."

"What now?"

Angie groans. "You'll have to go on your own because I'm due to leave for work in ten minutes."

Angie works at the Pigeon Trail, which is a pub on the outskirts of Granthaven. It merely reminds me that I also need to look for a job because the job offers must have been delayed in the post because I've had nothing back from the zillions of letters I've sent. It's actually soul destroying and my future plan of world domination is now uncertain.

"It's fine. I'll head back there. Karen may still be around."

"If she's not, ask Bert. He's probably taking a break in the potting shed. I heard he spends most of his time in there these days."

We share a grin because Bert has a man cave set up there with a woodburner among other things and enjoys many a happy hour drinking brandy, lager and anything else he can squirrel away while watching football on his phone.

I sigh heavily as I spy my boots by the door, hating the thought of leaving the warm fire to head back into the frosty winter.

"I should be going, anyway." I sigh.

"But mum said you could stay here."

Angie adds. "Make sure you come back later. It's too cold to stay at home alone."

"I'll see."

I smile, but we already know I'll be spending the

night in my own freezing attic room as always. Despite the fact I adore Angie's family, their house is small, like all the cottages in the village are, and I feel bad for imposing on them.

We leave together and as Angie dives into her small car and offers a prayer to the god of minis that it starts, I wave her goodbye and head back down the frozen path toward the lake.

Despite the fact I'm freezing, I love walking in winter. Granthaven has the most fantastic scenery, and it's doubtful I will meet anyone on my journey. We are a small community untouched by modern living and it's rather charming, if not a hard life to live.

As I head down the cobbled path by the side of the church, the wind blows, causing me to shiver in my cold wellington boots. I grasp my coat a little tighter around me and attempt to close any gaps for the icy wind to find its way through onto my already frozen skin.

The air is crisp and cold and every breath I take is full of oxygen, with no contamination. That is the advantage of living here. Nothing pollutes our glorious countryside outside of Bert's petrol lawn mower or his quad bike.

Everything is quiet and still, only the occasional rustling of the remaining leaves in the trees disturbing the peace. I head through the gap in the hedge and down the grassy embankment towards the partially frozen lake that glistens under the weak winter sun.

I stop for a minute and admire the intricate patterns that have formed on the ice, nature's own blank canvas to decorate at will. Even the ducks have sought shelter from the elements, their usual company nowhere to be found.

My nose is frozen and my cheeks sting as the winter

chill grips my face in its icy fingers. My feet no longer have any sensation in them, so I reluctantly carry on my journey.

I ignore the sign that warns me this land is private and to keep out because the villagers stopped taking notice of them years ago. Lady Townsend always encouraged us to delight in her gardens, something we were extremely grateful for.

As I approach the huge manor house, it appears even colder than it did this morning. It's an austere building that rises majestically from the landscape, dominating the skyline and reminding me of my station in life. My thoughts turn to the new owner and I wonder what he will think of it. Come to think of it, I wonder about the new owner because out of curiosity I searched for him online and knew immediately he wouldn't last five minutes here.

He has a celebrity girlfriend and a life that the rest of us can only imagine, and yet as I studied him closer I saw the twinkle in his eyes as he smiled at the camera. He is certainly good looking, a little too good looking, and I hate the interest I have in him. If I'm honest, I hate to fangirl over anyone unless you count the Hemsworth brothers. They deserve all the adulation they can get.

I near the huge front door and wonder if I should just inch it open, but I'm not sure if the new owners are here yet and the last thing I want is to be caught trespassing – well, indoors, anyway.

I ring the huge iron bell pull that must be ancient by now and as the bell jangles, I stamp my frozen feet and blow on my fingers in an attempt to warm them up.

I listen for footsteps but hear nothing and a shiver

runs down my spine as an icy blast catches me off-guard. I ring the bell again, more in desperation than anything, because it now appears that retrieving my phone is the most important thing in my life. I may miss someone phoning with a job offer, and I will lose out because my phone isn't glued to my hand like it should be.

I almost give up before I detect the dragging of a bolt on the other side of the door and my heart rate increases as I prepare to apologise for disturbing whoever is on the other side.

As the door opens, I take a step back because I wasn't expecting it to be *him*.

Luke Adams himself.

The new owner and the new star of my wandering imagination stands before me in all his glory.

I hate that there is an immediate spark of attraction that warms me far more effectively than any of my previous attempts and I openly stare at his warm smile that is drawing me in and rendering me speechless.

"Hi."

His voice is deep, smooth and almost caressing and I'm sure my face is flaming right now, as well as my libido.

"Um, hi."

My voice is nowhere near as smooth and seductive, rather high and squeaky if I'm honest and I shift awkwardly on the spot, wishing like crazy that Karen had opened the door.

"Can I help you?"

He is speaking, but I don't register his words as I gaze at his chiselled face, his cheekbones a master stroke of God's genius and a strong jawline that is slightly shaded by dark stubble. His eyes are a deep chestnut brown –

like acorns – that have a warmness that draws me in and holds me captive. His slightly bushy eyebrows are raised in a quizzical expression, reminding me he asked me a question and I say awkwardly, "I'm, um, sorry to disturb you but I was, um, here earlier and think I left my phone behind."

"Earlier?" He arches his brow and I stumble over my words.

"Yes, um, in the bedrooms. I mean, making the beds, playing housekeeper, you, um, know the kind of thing."

Another icy blast catches me off-guard and he angles his head and opens the door wider. "Come in, it's bloody freezing out there."

Never has a sentence made me react so fast and I waste no time in pushing through the door into a hallway that is no warmer than the porch outside.

I notice his face is also a little pinched, and he is shivering, despite the huge padded jacket he is wearing.

"I'm sorry, you must have just arrived and I'm disturbing you."

I apologise, glancing around for any other sign of life.

He chuckles softly and I now understand the power of this man as his smile could light up a room and reveals an incredibly handsome man. His teeth are perfectly aligned and gleaming white, a mastery of dentistry that doesn't come cheap and his lips are full and inviting and curled in a genuine, friendly smile that is doing a very good job of putting me at ease.

"No, actually I've been here for hours, but I can't get warm. Perhaps we should continue this conversation in the living room. There's a fire going great guns in there and I'm definitely sleeping in there tonight."

I follow him nervously, every step I take full of curiosity and intrigue concerning this man. I am taken aback by him because I never expected him to be so, well, normal, in a male model, completely out of my league kind of way.

I follow him, hating the turbulent thoughts running through my mind right now and as we reach the living room, I almost groan at the sudden burst of hot air that wafts across my face as he opens the door.

"Come in. I'd say take your coat off, but that would be certain suicide."

He laughs and I'm mesmerised by the deep rich rumble that comes from his throat, all husky and masculine and devastating for my heart.

He points to a dusty threadbare chair and winks, causing my heart to dive into free-fall.

"Take a seat and tell me where you think you left your phone."

As the flames flicker and crackle in the grate, the warmth from his personality as well as the fire makes me relax a little and as I sink into the chair, he takes the one opposite and for a brief moment in time, my world is perfect.

CHAPTER 6
LUKE

Not many things stun me, but my mysterious visitor has. When I saw her frozen smile at my door, a flicker of warmth melted a piece of my jaded heart. Her big blue luminous eyes stared at me with curiosity, the long dark lashes dusting her cheeks as she blinked in surprise. Her face was pale due to the cold, like porcelain, and her soft full lips were as red as the berries on the nearby holly bush.

She is wearing a bright red bobble hat and what appears to be a hand knitted scarf and the padded coat she is wearing is only just adequate against the elements. She is adorable and definitely the brightest star in this dismal night sky, and inviting her in was as easy as breathing.

"I'm Luke."

I offer her my hand, more as an excuse to touch hers and she says awkwardly, "Jessy."

"I'm pleased to meet you, Jessy."

I hold her frozen hand in my slightly warmer one and

smile into her eyes, noting the spark of interest in return, giving me hope that all is not lost.

"Do you live nearby?" I groan at my stupid question because it's doubtful she would just be passing as we're miles away from anywhere.

"Yes. All my life, regrettably."

"Why regrettably?"

It hasn't escaped either of our attention that I am still holding onto her hand and her breath hitches as she laughs with apprehension.

"I'm guessing you are wondering about this place. I expect your usual home is in the city, or at least has central heating."

She withdraws her hand with an embarrassed smile and glances around her.

"This is a beautiful room."

"Is it?"

I'm surprised, and she smiles dreamily.

"I can sense the history of this place." It's all around us and I imagine many ghosts are circling us now."

"I sincerely hope not." I laugh and she blushes furiously.

"I suppose, but don't you love the fact it's remained in the past? Untouched by modern living. I mean, there aren't many places these days that transport you back to the past, a virtual time machine if you like."

I shrug and with a sigh take my seat, the heavy surgical boot on my foot making me clumsy. I note her peering at it with interest and say with a deep sigh, "I broke my ankle. I'm recuperating."

"Did it hurt?"

Her eyes widen with concern, and I nod. "A little, but it could have been worse."

"Could it?"

"It might have been my leg, which would require a longer recovery time."

She shivers and I note the logs burning to nothing and lean across and attempt to throw a nearby one on the fire. It falls into the grate and she rolls her eyes.

"It's a good job you're not a cricketer."

She kneels down, expertly stacking the logs from a basket by the side and says, "I was sorry to hear of your injury, but even sorrier to hear of your aunt's passing."

Well, that's put things into perspective and I feel bad.

"Thank you."

She glances in my direction and then blushes as she looks away and I ask, "Tell me about yourself, Jessy."

She rocks back on her heels and holds her hands up in front of the gentle flame to try to warm them.

"I've lived in Granthaven my entire life, only leaving to attend university in Newcastle."

"Why there?"

"Why not?" She fixes me with a frown.

"I've never been north before and was interested. It has a rich history, and the university offered an amazing course on business."

"Is that what you graduated with, a business degree?"

"Yes."

She sits back in her seat and smiles. "It fascinates me. It's so complicated, like picking up a thread and seeing where it leads. Decisions may make millions or cost millions, depending on how things pan out."

"So, you're a gambler then?"

"Not in the usual sense."

She shrugs and peers around and I watch the nerves return.

"I'm sorry, I'm taking up your time. Perhaps I should retrieve my phone and leave you to settle in."

"Stay." The word falls out of my mouth before I can stop it and she raises her eyes.

"Stay?"

I shrug in a stupid attempt to regain some kind of cool.

"I mean, this is my first night and I have many questions. You're a local and likely able to answer most of them.

"What do you want to know?"

The fire is now doing its job and I note the healthier glow to her skin, a pink tinge that offsets the sparkle in her beautiful eyes.

"I've seen the house. Not all of it but what I've seen doesn't fill me with confidence."

"What do you mean?"

"Well, it's hardly, um, comfortable, wouldn't you agree?"

She smiles. "It must have been a shock."

"What, the décor or the fact it's mine at all?"

"Both I'm guessing."

"It was."

I glance at the photograph of Aunt Christabel that sits on a dusty piano.

"I never really knew my aunt, which is why it was a surprise."

"She was an amazing woman."

I note the softening in her expression as she smiles sadly.

"I didn't know her very well, but she was kind and wanted the best for the village. She was a lovely landlady, despite the fact she didn't have a clue on how to run the estate."

"In what way?"

She blushes and says quickly, "I'm sorry, that was disrespectful."

"No, tell me."

She heaves a deep breath and sighs. "This house is no different from any other in Granthaven, although they have fewer rooms. I mean–" She waves her hand at the dusty décor. "They are all in need of repair, have no central heating, just old fireplaces and the roofs need re-tiling. The grounds were left to nature, and the church is in dire need of restoration along with the village hall. Granthaven was once a thriving village but is seriously now in danger of extinction."

"Wow, tell me how it is. Don't spare my feelings." I stare at her in shock and for some reason she laughs out loud.

"Well, you did ask."

It strikes me that there is something so incredibly enticing about Jessy. From the moment I opened the door, I felt it. She is definitely attractive, pretty and sweet, but I detect an underlying steel inside her that tells me she's smarter than most people would give her credit for.

She regards me curiously. "You have a mammoth task ahead of you if you want this place to continue."

"Not really."

I shrug, dismissing the problem out of hand.

"Why not?"

"Because I'm selling up as soon as the year is up. I'm only here to see what I inherited, and I have absolutely no intention of making it my home."

Silence falls like a judge's gavel and she stares at me with disappointment that, for some reason, is like a blow to my heart.

"I see." She stands and her eyes flash as she says firmly, "Then I'll bid you good evening and retrieve my phone. Thank you for your hospitality, but I should be heading home."

"Wait."

She heads to the door and as she wrenches it open, a blast of cold air causes the fire to flicker in the grate.

She doesn't even wait and slams the door closed behind her and I can't even hurry after her because my stupid boot tips the side table over.

By the time I reach the door, she is nowhere to be seen and I'm guessing she went to get her phone. However, the slamming of the front door tells me she either left it where it was, or found it on her way out.

I'm not sure why, but I feel like Prince Charming watching Cinderella run off and it's as if something important has happened. I don't know what I said that was so bad. I mean, surely nobody really believes I'm going to live here. Why would they? I live in Manchester. My job and my life are there. It makes perfect sense to sell this place and let whoever buys it turn it around.

Not me.

Definitely not me and if Jessy what's her name thought any different, then she is sadly mistaken.

CHAPTER 7
JESSY

The worst thing about storming off in a huff is the only person bothered about that is me. I left my stupid phone behind, which was the entire reason for my visit in the first place.

I stomp back down the path toward the lake, muttering curses about Luke flaming Adams under my breath. What a moron. A stupid, clueless, gorgeously handsome idiot, who I definitely hate right now. His arrogance infuriates me, even though his kindness is all I can think of when I picture his soft smile cast in my direction.

I am conflicted, angry, and God damn it – interested.

I give myself a stern talking to as I march home.

He is insufferable.

He is arrogant.

He is stupid.

He is gorgeous.

Aargh. Why did I ever go there? Now I can't erase his

image from my mind or those burning eyes and hot sexy winks he throws around like love darts. His seriously wicked smile and tender hold make my heart beat faster. He is everything he appears and more, and yet I have no business being attracted and repelled by him in equal measure.

He has a girlfriend, for goodness' sake. A celebrity one at that, and his hospitality was just a way of passing the time.

I left my freaking phone behind.

I can't believe I was so stupid and now I must invent a reason and a way to get it back without him knowing.

To make matters worse, my home is like walking into a freezer and there will definitely be no hot water. I haven't eaten and there is no food in the house, unless you count a stale loaf of bread and handful of nuts as a sumptuous feast.

I scream inside my head and picture Angie's home lit like a Christmas tree and throwing out serious heat from the wood-burning stove and I sigh. I should go there and take advantage of their hospitality and first thing in the morning get my own house in order.

~

"He said what?"

Angie's face is etched in horror as I relay the events that happened yesterday. I was asleep when she returned home after the pub closed and as soon as I took my first breath this morning, it was to rant about the celebrity who is about to ruin our lives.

The night the mistletoe died 43

"He's selling up!"

Angie appears as worried as I am, and I nod miserably. "One year. That's all he has to keep it for and then he'll sell to the highest bidder and wander back to Manchester with several million pounds in his bank."

"This is a disaster."

Angie is spot on because it is. It's everyone's greatest fear that a huge multi-national company will buy Granthaven and change it forever. The manor house will become a hotel, or a conference centre. The houses will either be sold off to second home seekers from London, or the rents will increase to market rates, effectively putting most of out on the street. It is the worst threat this village has ever faced and I hate that if the man responsible winked in my general direction, I would forgive him in a heartbeat.

"What are we going to do?"

"I don't know."

I take a deep breath and change direction.

"Angie."

"What?"

"I don't suppose you can head up there and get my phone. In my anger, I stomped off and left it there."

"I'm on it."

Angie is out of the door quicker than a greyhound in a trap, and I smile to myself. She just can't wait to check him out for herself and, knowing my friend, give him a piece of her mind while she's at it.

I head across to the frosted window and watch her running down the street, a heavy padded coat gently brushing against the top of her walking boots, and a woolly hat pulled down firmly on her head. I wonder if Luke Adams will discover that she is wearing a onesie underneath. It's the only thing that keeps us warm in our beds at night and we celebrate the creator of them. There are no slinky nightdresses in Granthaven in the middle of winter. Thermal socks and underwear under a onesie are standard.

I dress in record speed, loathe to use any of their hot water while I shower and head down to breakfast where Margery is frying bacon in the kitchen, the woodburner already giving out serious heat. The scent of coffee and smoky bacon fills my senses, and her warm smile earns one of my own back.

"Did you sleep well, love?"

"Like a log thanks Margery."

I am lying because I slept fitfully if I'm honest. A certain cheeky wink and soft smile heating my blood far more effectively than the thermals I slept in.

"Where did Angie go in such a hurry? I thought Harry Styles must be visiting."

She winks, causing me to laugh because Angie has an extremely soft spot for the man in question.

"She went to retrieve my phone from the manor house."

"Ah, now I see the urgency."

She flips the bacon and grins. "If it's not the dashing footballer who made her run faster than an Olympic sprinter, it's to take a look at her idol – that Morgana woman."

I hadn't considered that and in Angie's case was probably more of a temptation than Luke Adams. She is addicted to Morgana's podcasts, Instagram and TikTok feeds and is her number one fan, and once again my heart sinks when I picture the happy couple together. I could never compete with that and I should forget I ever met Luke flaming Adams.

∼

One bacon sandwich and a mug of coffee later, Angie bursts through the door, clutching my phone in her gloved hand.

"Got it!" She is out of breath and her cheeks are glowing, and Margery pours some coffee into her usual mug and nods toward the fire.

"Here you go, lovely. Drink this while I make you a sandwich."

"Thanks mum."

Angie shrugs off her coat and boots and presses the phone into my hand and groans.

"Just my luck."

"What is?"

"Bloody Karen Sims was there. Apparently, there is nobody home and the fires have long since burned out. Bert is currently grumbling about wasting logs as he sets about lighting them again."

"So you didn't see Luke?" I ask, a little disappointed not to have Angie's view of him and she shakes her head.

"No, Karen told me she arrived to see if he needed anything from the store. There can't have been much in the house and she thought he must be starving."

"I wonder where he is?"

I'm mystified, although the house is certainly big enough to lose yourself in, so I'm not overly concerned.

I glance at my phone and frown because there is a slip of paper sticking out from the phone case that definitely wasn't there yesterday.

As I pull it out, I note a few words and a telephone number.

"What's that?" Angie asks, as she sips her steaming mug of coffee.

"A note."

"Well, obviously." She rolls her eyes. "What does it say?"

"Call me."

"No way."

Angie leans forward to take a look and gasps, "You've only got Luke frigging Adam's phone number. Most girls would kill for that. You could sell it online and make a fortune."

"I may just do that."

With an angry frown, I screw up the paper and toss it into the fire and Angie yells, "Stop! What are you doing?"

"Why do I want to speak to that man? I am so angry with him."

Margery turns and stares at me in surprise.

"Why? What happened?"

I fill her in and she gasps, "That's terrible. This will affect everyone in Granthaven. He can't just write us off without knowing about this place first. He can't."

"Can't what?"

Angie's dad, Peter Barnes, heads into the room, and Margery fills him in on the story and he sighs deeply.

"I was afraid that would happen."

"We must stop him, Peter." Margery says, and I hate the worried gleam in her eye.

"I doubt we can influence him, love. These footballers think of nothing but the game and the next flash car."

I stare at the burning note in the fire and determination settles around me. Somebody has got to try at least and if we're going down, it won't be without a fight.

CHAPTER 8
LUKE

I feel bad. Very bad and I'm not sure why. It must be because I admitted defeat and caught a cab to join the others at the hotel soon after Jessy left. The lure of a hot bath and a decent meal was too great, and I joined them in time for dinner, over which we drew up plans to make this stay a little more comfortable.

Morgana's idea was to operate from the five-star country hotel that Steven secured for us. Jasper was also keen, but I had other ideas.

Now Jasper and Morgana are discussing interiors and renovations, leaving me to think about what happened yesterday.

I'm experiencing an emotion I've never had before.

Guilt.

I'm not sure what happened, but one minute I was enjoying the company of a woman who intrigued me and the next she stormed out of Granthaven Manor, minus the very thing she went there for. I only said I was selling up and I'm surprised at her reaction. Who wouldn't sell up? The place is a crumbling ruin and I'm not about to lose any sleep over it.

But I did.

Images of her freezing in the uncared for cottage that I now own, played on my mind while I enjoyed the comforts only five-star living can bring you. I pictured her shivering under her duvet while she thought up ways to kill me by drowning me in the frozen lake, probably.

Images of her beautiful, innocent eyes, shrouded in disbelief that changed from soft interest to downright hatred in a nanosecond, kept me awake and even now I am unaware of the reason.

"What do you say, Luke?"

Morgana's shrill voice drags my mind back to the present, and I shrug. "About?"

"Honestly, Luke, weren't you even listening?"

She shakes her head in disappointment and I'm kind of getting used to that reaction since coming here.

"The renovations. Jasper knows of a company who kit out rooms for television. They could do the same for the manor house and make it appear like a scene out of Downton Abbey. It might work and nobody would discover the real state of the place."

"Is it expensive?"

I'm loathe to spend any money on a place that would probably absorb it quicker than water on a dry sponge, and Steven pipes up, "Early estimates are one hundred thousand pounds."

"Then no."

I'm blunt, causing Morgana to throw up her hands in exasperation.

"Honestly, Luke. That money would be an investment

that will reap huge rewards. Just think about it, hun. Sponsorship deals, advertising revenue, potential visitors – I mean, we could open the house to the public when we've finished and open a tea room and everything. One hundred thousand is the tip of the iceberg with the revenue you may claw back in return."

I must admit she has a point, but then again, Morgana always has had an eye for business, which returns my attention to another business major with long blonde hair and sparkling blue eyes.

I finish up my breakfast and experience a sudden urge to return to Granthaven. It began as a dull ache inside me when I opened my eyes this morning and has been gaining in momentum ever since. I want to go back. To take another look at the place and this time wander away from the manor and into a world where a woman like Jessy lives.

I check my phone, but she hasn't called. There are many other calls, but none from her. When she left, I went in search of her and discovered her phone on the vanity unit in the bathroom on the first floor and even the pink unicorn on the case made me smile.

I tried to gain access to the phone to call one of her contacts, but all I managed to do was to remove the case, noting the number scrawled inside as a reminder to her. I smiled because it's a practical thing to do and doesn't surprise me in the slightest. She gave me that impression and so I programmed it into my phone under her name and slipped the note inside for her to call me.

I did consider keeping the phone so she would have to collect it from me, but decided it was a little obsessive, even for me.

The night the mistletoe died 51

She hasn't called and I hate the despair I'm experiencing as I glance at the phone, wishing her number would flash up with a text or anything.

Another woman does call me and as I answer the phone, the cool tones of the housekeeper, Karen, remind me of my responsibilities.

"Mr Adams. It's Karen Sims from Granthaven."

"Ah, yes, good morning."

"Will you be returning today? If so, I will instruct Bert to light the fires."

"Um, yes, thanks."

Once again, I feel bad because I am causing these people work that they probably can do without, and she asks quickly, "What about food?" I could organise some supplies from the local supermarket. Do you have a list?"

"Please, um, whatever you think will be fine."

I glance across at Steven, who is busy texting, and say quickly, "I'll pass you over to my agent. He will arrange payment and discuss our requirements."

Steven glances up and I roll my eyes and yet just before I hand him the phone, I say quickly, "I, um, don't suppose we had any visitors this morning."

"Well, yes, as it happens."

She sounds surprised and my heart strangely starts racing as I wait for her next words.

"One of the women who helped make the house ready yesterday left her phone behind and her friend came to retrieve it this morning."

My heart falls. "I see."

I'm not certain why I feel so bad but it won't go away and I even surprise myself by saying quickly, "Mrs Sims, um, how do I go about arranging a village meeting?"

Steven peers at me sharply as Morgana and Jasper continue their conversation, oblivious to anything other than mood boards.

"That would be through the chair of the resident's association, Mr Spalding." She says quickly and I take a deep breath and say decisively, "Please can you call him on my behalf and ask him to schedule it for one pm?"

"That's short notice, Mr Adams. I don't–"

I interrupt. "I know and I'm sorry, but I'm sure the villagers have many questions and I would like to address them."

"I'll see what I can do."

I hand the phone to Steven, who pointedly raises his eyes and I shrug, concealing my grin at the impatience in his expression as he says with an air of resignation, "Steven Chambers, Mrs Sims. Now about those supplies."

As the people surrounding me discuss spending my money, my thoughts turn to a pretty face that is sure to be my downfall. I glance across at Morgana chatting with animation to Jasper, and my heart sinks. Yes, Jessy of the beautiful blue eyes who now hates me with a passion, is trouble I can definitely do without but for some reason it is now the most important thing in my life to stare into them once again and change her opinion of me.

CHAPTER 9

JESSY

I note the group text on my phone from the WhatsApp group, Granthaven resident's association.

> Village meeting at 1 pm to meet the new owner of Granthaven, Mr Luke Adams.

My heart sinks. Just great.

I stare around the small cottage where I've lived my entire life and experience a twinge of sadness that life is changing so fast.

I returned home to make it ready for my parent's return and as I light the fire and set about cleaning, many memories dance around me like jovial ghosts from my past. I love living here and it's only now I'm faced with the possibility of moving on that I realise just how important this place is to me.

As I work, the flames from the fire breathe life into the place, chasing the cold away and replacing it with much needed warmth. The interior may be dated, but it is furnished with memories and my eyes fill with tears when I think back on happier times.

My parents don't have much, but what they have in abundance is love. For one another, for me and my sister Grace and not forgetting the village. They are currently celebrating their Pearl wedding anniversary and as a gift, the entire village contributed to a mini break in Vienna to visit the Christmas market there, and I know how touched they were.

That is the value of living here. Friends and a community who care. People who don't crave material possessions and live for shared moments of joy and friendship.

We are a team. The Granthaven family and faced with the possibility of that changing forever because of one spoilt man's decision, is too much to comprehend.

Christmas carols are playing on the radio and the fairy lights twinkle on the small tree in the corner of the room. I never appreciated how tenuous a moment can be. Even if that moment lasts for twenty-five plus years, it can be wiped away in the name of progress inside twenty-four hours.

Similar to the situation in nearby Tyneham, where the entire village was relocated during the war so the army could use their homes as target practice. They were assured they could return after the war had ended, but that never happened. Now we are facing similar ruin and I don't know what to do about that.

My thoughts return to Luke Adams and disappointment hits me hard. I thought he was kind.

I was wrong.

I suppose I was blinded by his soft glances in my direction and the sweet smile he threw my way. I was taken in as I'm sure many others have been before me and yet he is no different from any scoundrel. Now he has summoned the villagers to a meeting like the lord he thinks he is, no doubt to ruin our Christmas by telling us we have one year left of life as we know it.

Once again, the tears prick behind my eyes as I contemplate moving on. Life will never be the same again and it's all because one person controls the lives of this entire village and always has done.

∽

I HAVE HALF a mind not to go to his stupid meeting, but curiosity wins out and with a final check on the place, I close the door and turn the key, sure my parents will be home before I am. They called from the airport and are making their way home, and are now apparently approaching Dorchester, and I can't wait to hear every detail of their trip.

I'm surprised when I reach the village hall to find there are no spare seats left. In fact, I've never seen it so crowded and stare around in shock as it appears the entire village is here, not to mention a few strangers.

Angie waves at me from the back of the room.

"Over here, Jessy. We saved you a space against the wall."

I edge through the grumbling bodies until I reach the small space reserved for me and Angie says, wide-eyed, "I'm guessing everyone wants a peek at the celebrities. I don't recognise half of these people, do you?"

"I've never seen them before."

I'm a little bemused because this shouldn't be

allowed. It's an important meeting concerning our village, not a free for all to gaze upon the rich footballer and his influencer girlfriend. If she bothers to come, that is.

Angie nudges me as the door opens and the noise levels increase as Luke enters the hall, appearing a little stunned by the sheer number of people here.

Angie gasps, "Wow, he's gorgeous. It's a shame I didn't get here earlier. I would love a place at the front."

"So would everyone else, it seems."

The only good thing about the crowd is that they warm up the room and act as a human wall between me and the guy I detest with a passion.

The worst thing of all is the fact my heart actually fluttered when he arrived, his designer scarf wound tightly around his neck and his black padded jacket more than adequate in keeping the chill away.

Angie nudges me sharply in the ribs as another person follows him inside, along with another man who stares around him with an air of boredom. A third man also joins them and appears to be filming the whole charade and I clench my fists as they make their way to the front of the hall to stand on a small stage.

"She is gorgeous."

Angie's voice is awestruck as she gazes with hero worship at Morgana, who is a vision in a fur bandana with a matching fur jacket over velvet leggings. Her long blonde hair is curled to her shoulders and her bright red painted lips are resting in amusement as she faces the crowd, secure in the knowledge that she is the most glamorous woman in the room. The other man stands by her side like a bodyguard and if I've envied anyone in my life, it is nothing compared to how much I envy that woman as she gazes at Luke and smiles her encouragement.

I wish like hell I had never come because I can't tear my eyes away from the man standing awkwardly at the front of his adoring public that could well turn into a lynch mob when they discover what his plans are.

CHAPTER 10
LUKE

This was a bad idea. A monumentally bad one and could end badly for me. Why didn't I think this through? It appears every person in the village is crowded inside this building and they are staring at me as if I'm an alien who has landed.

I clear my throat and say loudly, "Um, thank you for coming at such short notice."

A gentle murmur accompanies my words, and I scan the crowd for the only face I want to see in it. This whole idea was to flush Jessy out and force her to listen to me. To replace the loathing in her eyes and to engineer some more time in her company.

I see nothing but the usual adoration and I swallow hard.

"As you may have heard, I am the new owner of Granthaven – for my sins."

I roll my eyes, but nobody is laughing and so I quickly cough and say brightly. "My Aunt Christabel has entrusted the estate to me and I'm a little overwhelmed, if I'm honest."

Morgana rests her hand on my arm in a show of support and I'm glad of it. She wanted to be here, solidarity in numbers she called it, but I'm guessing it was to demonstrate how close we are to the camera that is recording every minute of my excruciating speech for Jasper's reality show.

"So, um, I just wanted to meet you all and ask for your help."

A gentle murmur accompanies my words and I note a few encouraging smiles from the audience as I cough and say quickly, "I find it difficult to run my house, let alone all of yours, so please forgive me while I get to grips with what that means. So–"

Once again, I scan the crowd, but I still can't find Jessy and my heart sinks.

"So, um, I was hoping to work with you all and learn what it is I've inherited. Mrs Sims – Karen–" I gesture to Karen who is sitting in the front row, "Has kindly drawn up a questionnaire that I would ask you to fill in, along with a list of your names, addresses and any suggestions or problems that you have. Her friend Valerie will assist her, and I promise I will look at them all and try to help."

Morgana steps forward and smiles at the crowd and I register a sea of phones pointed in her direction.

"Luke and I are super excited to be here and can't wait to get stuck in. Please be assured that we have your best interests at heart, but ask for your patience while we settle in."

A few people start clapping and I use the distraction to scan the crowd some more but come up empty and a wave of frustration hits me as I conclude that this has been a complete waste of time.

Where is she?

Steven steps in and holds up his hand and says loudly, "We will be in touch once the questionnaires have been filled in. Please see Karen and Valerie and return them to the village hall post box when completed."

Karen and Valerie stand, which I take as my cue to leave and as we file out of the hall, the noise levels increase as several questions are shouted into the air.

As we step outside, Morgana giggles. "That was such fun."

I don't reply because the crowd surges after us and we are soon swamped with people wanting photos and autographs that Morgana is only too happy to oblige them with, while I desperately scan the sea of faces that leave the hall for one very important one.

I almost miss her but note her red bobble hat and my heart beats faster as she turns and heads the other way.

"Excuse me, um, sorry."

I start pushing my way through the crowd, desperate to reach her, but she is fast, and the crowd is difficult to negotiate and the freaking boot on my foot is making my progress difficult.

"Jessy!"

One word said at the highest volume causes the crowd to quiet immediately and all eyes turn to the direction my voice went as I shout again, "Jessy, wait!"

She either doesn't hear me or pretends not to and quickens her pace without looking back.

"JESSY!"

I'm shocked as the crowd roars her name and they

must hear it from Dorchester, which means she has no choice but to stop and turn around slowly.

It's as if I part the Sea of Galilee as the crowd splits in two, allowing me safe passage and as I make my way through the curious glances and register the sea of phones all pointing in our direction, not to mention Jasper's, I am conscious I just made life extremely difficult for myself.

I've gone too far now though and as I stumble toward her, I note the frozen expression in her eye that was placed there by me and not the weather, and I smile apologetically.

"Please, let me explain."

Her eyes move past me and I'm conscious of the silent crowd staring and then she nods towards the path she was set upon.

"Follow me. We can talk over there."

At least she said talk. That's something at least and as I limp along behind her, I don't give a second thought to any explanations.

We move behind a set of trees that conceal us from the crowd and as I reach her, she turns and shoves her hands in her pockets and says coolly, "You said it all yesterday, unless you've changed your mind, of course."

"I'm sorry if I offended you."

"Offended me?" She rolls her eyes. "You write off my history – Granthaven's legacy in one conceited, ill-judged sentence and expect me to forgive you just because you asked people to fill out a questionnaire that you will probably file in the bin after deciding it's not worth your trouble."

She shakes her head and her anger stabs me straight in the heart.

"I'm sorry, Luke. You are entitled to do what you like with Granthaven and I get that you don't want this. You have another life, one that I'm sure you've worked pretty hard to get and I'm being hard on you."

I sense her anger evaporating slowly and she shifts on the spot, hunching her shoulders as if in defeat.

"Just do what you want. It's no business of mine."

"But it could be." I say quickly, causing her to raise her eyes and stare at me with confusion.

"What do you mean?"

"It means I need an advisor. Somebody who knows this place, how it operates and the people it concerns. Somebody who has just graduated with a business degree, looking for work who may have all the required enthusiasm and a hunger to succeed."

She stares at me in shock as I say desperately, "Somebody who would demand a salary of, well, fifty thousand pounds, to devote all her time to helping an arrogant jerk learn what he is in danger of letting slip through his fingers. Somebody like you, Jessy."

"But–" She steps back, confusion etched in her frown lines.

"Why me? You could employ a person way more qualified than me."

"But I want you."

I hate the needy desperation in my voice that I can't even explain to myself. There is something telling me that I need Jessy more than anyone else right now and I don't have the first clue why.

CHAPTER 11
JESSY

I must be dreaming. This can't be happening, but the expression on Luke's face tells me he's deadly serious.

Fifty thousand pounds a year.

I can't believe it. It's so much money; more than I ever thought I'd earn in my first job and it would be working for him.

His dark brown eyes are brimming with hope and his soft smile is like kryptonite to my heart. He wants me. Jessy Potter. But why?

"Please, Jessy. I need you."

I'm lost for words and then we hear a loud, "Luke, darling."

Luke's face falls and a flash of exasperation crosses his features as he groans, "Morgana."

"Your girlfriend." I remind him and he shrugs.

"Will you do it, Jessy? Please say yes."

"Why the change of heart from yesterday?"

I'm confused and wonder if the ghost of Aunt Christabelle somehow haunted him in his sleep and changed the direction of his thought process. It can only be that and I'm surprised when he grips my arm and says desperately, "Come back with me. I'll introduce you as a member of my team and we can begin to unravel this mess and hopefully make everybody happy."

I am so conflicted. Part of me wants to tell him to shove his job up his newly acquired back passage, but the other part of me is seduced by his offer. By him actually and as for the money, I would be a fool to turn that down, so I nod reluctantly.

"It wouldn't hurt to discover the details."

He exhales sharply and then smiles, and it's as if the sun comes out and melts my frozen heart.

"You will. Thank God. Come on, it's not a great idea to keep Morgana waiting for too long."

Even the mention of her name is a bullet to my fragile heart, and yet this is business. It's a job offer, nothing else, just employment. The trouble is, now I'll have to witness first-hand how a man like Luke Adams acts around the woman he loves and the knowledge that woman will never be me.

WE HEAD BACK around the trees and I shrink away from the curious glances that greet us. Luke smiles reassuringly and says rather loudly so everyone can hear, "Jessy is my business advisor for Granthaven. I'm so glad I caught her. We have a lot of work to do."

I note the relief in Morgana's eyes as she smiles at me sweetly, and then I notice the shock in the eyes of the man accompanying them.

"Steven." Luke waves him over and turns to me.

"Steven Chambers is my agent and good friend. He will help you with anything you need."

He points to the other man. "That's Jasper. He's producing our reality show. He may ask you to participate, but that's up to you."

Jasper waves from his position on the sidelines as he films every move Morgana makes, and as we near the woman herself, she holds out her hand and says warmly. "I'm so pleased to meet you, Jessy. If you have any questions at all, please ask me, and if I don't know, I can point you in the direction of someone who might."

It's now official. I'm in hell because Morgana appears to be the sweetest woman alive, and I am lusting after her boyfriend. How will this work? It will end up breaking me, but as I glance around at the familiar faces surrounding us, I know I must give this my best shot. If I can save the future of this village by applying everything I've learned, it will be worth every minute of being in the presence of a group of people who make my head and heart spin.

While I wait for Luke and Morgana to manage the crowds, Angie finds me and pulls me to one side.

"What's going on?"

Her eyes are wide as she nods in Luke's direction.

"He offered me a job."

"I get that, but why?"

"I don't know."

We stare at one another in complete shock and she shakes her head in disbelief.

"This is a life-changing moment, Jessy."

"You're so melodramatic." I laugh nervously.

"No it is. I mean, working for Luke Adams. It's a dream come true."

"I suppose it is, but what if it all goes wrong?" I whisper, glancing at the man himself as he takes a selfie with a group of fans.

"Then you will have a good memory to keep you warm at night." Angie grins. "I mean, way to go Jessy. What happened back there was the stuff of movies and I saw that man with the camera filming every moment of it."

"For their reality TV show, nothing else."

I roll my eyes. "I expect he's doing this as a publicity stunt."

"In what way?"

Angie's expression is fierce, which makes me smile.

"Think about it. He knows he must keep Granthaven in the family for one year. It would be a lonely, turbulent year if the village is against him, or it could be a PR opportunity."

Angie's face falls. "I see where you're going with this."

"Outwardly, it appears he has done everything possible to make this work and even employed somebody in the village to help him, using her as a scapegoat when things don't work out. Shifting the blame onto her when he is forced to sell up because she couldn't find a way to make it work."

She glances at the happy couple and frowns. "Genius really. Despicable but genius."

I follow her gaze and say with determination. "Then we must make certain it does work and show him that Granthaven is worth his investment. That it's an asset he would be a fool to dispose of and the people here are special and are deserving of a second chance."

"If anyone can change his mind, I'm sure it's you J." she says warmly.

I catch Luke's eye and he grins and I swear my heart crashes and burns. Something is telling me this will be a fight I may lose and it won't just be my home that's under threat. My heart may never recover and my well-ordered life will fall like a pack of cards in a stiff breeze.

CHAPTER 12
LUKE

Jessy is silent as she follows us back to the manor house and I expect it's because Morgana is clutching my arm and whispering in my ear as we walk.

"That went well, hun. You had them eating out of your hand."

"I suppose."

She snuggles into my side. "This may not be so bad after all."

"How do you work that one out? Because from where I'm standing, we are in an impossible situation."

I point to the house looming up before us like an albatross around my neck. "Look at this place. It needs to be bulldozed and re-built at a cost of millions. Then there are the properties I now own. Apparently, they have no central heating and are in a bad state of disrepair. As the landlord, I am required to bring them up to a standard that will cost several more millions that I don't possess."

"But you could."

"How do you work that one out?"

I shiver as the icy wind whips around my face and it wouldn't be so bad if the house we are heading to was warm.

"Think about it, Luke. We are in a great position to draw in the crowds. Sponsorship even. I could use my platform to renovate the house and the properties."

Her voice rises as the excitement grips her.

"I was speaking about it with Jasper over breakfast. He is so on board with this, Luke. We use the reality show to renovate Granthaven. It will be called 'Saving Granthaven' and we will get sponsors and everything. This may be just what we need while you're out of action and it may even make us more money in the long run."

She does make a good point and I can't say I'm surprised because Morgana has made a career out of utilising social media and many underestimate her business acumen.

"What does Steven say?" I ask because knowing Morgana, she has run every aspect of this through him first.

"Of course he agrees with me." She giggles and throws an amused smile in the direction of our agent, who is now deep in conversation with Jessy as they follow us.

I am monetarily distracted by her and something tugs on my heartstrings when I notice the expression in her eyes. She is pale, understandable in winter, but there is a weariness about her that tells me she's suffering somehow. I cast my mind back to our conversation yesterday, that changed after one unguarded comment. This place is her life, and she is worried. I can see it in her eyes and I want to reassure her that I will help, but how can I?

I smile at Morgana. "If anybody can make this work, you can."

"You know it." She grins as she grips my arm a little tighter, and as we head up to the large oak door, she groans. "The first thing I'm changing is this bloody decrepit door."

"Leave it."

I stare at the ancient door with a strong sense of nostalgia. "Actually, I kind of like its cracks and blemishes. It would be like burying a person who still has many amazing stories to tell."

"Oh, Luke." Morgana laughs out loud. "I can tell I'm going to have my work cut out with you."

We head inside and as the others follow us in, Morgana whispers, "That was a stroke of genius with Jessy."

"What do you mean?" I note Steven saying something to her that makes her giggle and I smile.

"Involving the locals with your business here. Bridging the gap between us and them. She seems lovely too, so yes, that was a good move."

As I catch Jessy's eye, I smile.

"I think so too."

Jasper heads across and sighs heavily.

"Okay, top priority. Let's heat this mausoleum and then we can think straight. I've got several storage heaters heading our way from the production company. They assured me they're nearby and will get them up and running in no time."

"When did you arrange that?" I stare at him in

surprise and he raises his eyes. "Yesterday, as soon as I saw what I was working with."

Morgana nods. "Yes, Jasper has everything under control, and we begin filming after they arrive."

She nods towards Jessy. "Perhaps you should brief your recruit on how things work around here while I head off with Jasper and Steven to make some coffee. The home delivery should have arrived by now."

"What home delivery?"

I'm definitely missing part of my life somehow and Morgana says briskly, "We ordered it when we were at the hotel yesterday, along with new bedding and towels and other sundry items. Honestly Luke, if we are doing this, we are doing it properly and you may have buried your head in the sand, but Jasper, Steven and I have got you covered. Now go and sort things out with Jessy and we'll bring you some coffee as soon as we're organised."

She heads off with Jasper and I gaze after them in shock, but I don't know why I'm surprised really. Morgana takes her creature comforts extremely seriously and I doubt that is the last invoice I'll be paying before the day is out.

∽

JESSY IS NERVOUS. She is glancing around her like a rabbit caught in headlights as she sits once again in the threadbare chair by the fire.

This time the temperature is sufficient to enable us to discard our coats and I love the pale blue sweater she is wearing with a cat on the front. The colour reflects in her beautiful blue eyes and I can't help being mesmerised by her.

Maybe it's because I'm staring that she is uncomfortable, or it could be because I've sprung a situation on her that I haven't fully explained yet and so I say softly, "Thank you for hearing me out."

"Are you going to tell me what the offer was about?" She asks and I'm not sure I can answer that because it was a spur-of-the-moment decision just to get her to talk to me again. Now I've asked, I must honour my offer and say with a slight shrug, "It makes perfect sense. I need somebody to liaise between me and the villagers and after hearing of your degree, I wanted to pick your brains about this place."

She raises her eyes and I say quickly, "I mean, I want to make this work, but even you must admit it's a lot."

"I guess."

She sighs and stares into the flickering fire and smiles. "Granthaven has been my life ever since I can remember. It's a magical place, but even I must admit it's failing."

She holds out her hands and warms them against the fire and says with a wistful expression, "Lady Townsend tried, but when Lord Townsend died she was thrust into a world she never understood the first thing about. Their only income was from the rents and they are lower than average due to their generosity."

"So, I should put the rents up. I don't think that will go down well."

"You should, but no, it wouldn't."

She sighs and leans back, regarding me through those astonishing eyes, her lashes sweeping against her cheeks as she thinks. I'm surprised at my reaction to her because

I am often surrounded by attractive women but there is something different about Jessy.

As if on cue, Morgana enters the room with a huge silver tray, two mugs of steaming coffee and a plate of biscuits.

"Here you go. Fuel for the workers."

She hands one to Jessy and smiles sweetly. "I'm so glad Luke employed you. God knows I need another female opinion. It's hard work being the only creative one in the family."

She huffs and then winks as she hands a mug to me. "Don't be sore about that hun, you know I speak the truth."

It makes me chuckle. "You always do."

I glance at Jessy and roll my eyes. "If I didn't have Morgana, I wouldn't be half the man I am now. She tells me how it is and organises my life. You should get on."

Morgana grins and shakes her head as she peers around the room.

"Well, I say thank God for Jasper. He will soon make this place habitable. Now, if you'll excuse me, I must meet with him to discuss the way forward. I mean, we have a programme to make and that requires meticulous planning.

As she leaves, Jessy smiles and whispers, "Why do I like her so much?"

"Because she deserves it. Morgana doesn't possess a bad bone in her body and is the most generous, sweetest person I have ever met. You will learn a lot from her."

Jessy nods and sips her drink, but for some reason her eyes just lost a little of their sparkle.

CHAPTER 13
JESSY

I am so conflicted. I love Granthaven more than anything, but my fascination with Luke is unnerving me. He is very kind, but that is all. He loves another amazing woman, and I shouldn't think too much about a soft smile or a wistful glance in my direction. He is out of bounds and I must push aside this weird obsession I have for him and concentrate on doing the job he is paying me for.

We finish our drinks and he nods towards our coats that are in a heap on the faded settee.

"If you can stand it, I wonder if we could take a walk around the village. I'd like to see it and you'd make a great tour guide."

"Of course."

We pull on our coats and hats again and head off, our progress a little slower as he hobbles on his boot and I say with concern, "Does it hurt?"

"No, it's more awkward than anything. The boot

comes off next week, though, which will present a different set of problems."

"In what way?"

"On whether my foot will be strong enough to resume training."

"What if it's not?"

He shrugs. "Then this place will become home far sooner than planned."

I fall silent because I can tell the subject concerns him and as we head outside once again, I distract his mind away from one problem to another.

"You now own over two thousand acres, as I'm sure you're aware, but they require as much upkeep as the manor house, if not more."

"Any ideas?" He asks and I nod, my mind moving onto a subject that I have often contemplated long and hard about.

"There is a farm that brings in some revenue from the tenancy, but not much. Many other landowners set up shooting and country pursuits to encourage corporate clients. It pays well and is much-needed extra income."

He nods and I can tell I have his full attention.

"The house and surrounding gardens are perfect to offer film crews. They would pay to rent the space and be a good revenue stream. There is also the possibility of setting up a company providing wedding event hire. The church is in the perfect location for that, as it's adjacent to the house. For those who want a non-religious ceremony, the house has many rooms that are suitable, not to mention the various bedrooms for the wedding guests. Failing that, a marquee in the grounds would also work well."

He appears impressed. "I can tell you've been thinking about this – a lot."

"I did my dissertation on it if you must know."

"What grade did you get, out of interest?"

He winks and I hate how my heart beats a little faster.

"I achieved a first."

"If I knew what that was, I'd be impressed, I'm guessing."

It makes me giggle and as we pass the huge lake, he stops suddenly.

"Wow!"

I see the lake through his eyes. I'm guessing this is the first time he's seen the full extent of its majesty because half of it is hidden from the house. There is no other like it in Dorset, and the crystal clear water spills down to a small waterfall into a stream that runs the length of the village.

"It's impressive."

I nod. "It's magnificent."

I point to the clearing where a group of trees provide much-needed shade in the summer months.

"We receive many visitors here all year round, but mainly in the summer months. Picnics, walks, you know the kind of thing."

"I can see why."

He points to the fence separating the house from the lake, marked private.

"Is this all I have keeping the visitors out of my garden?"

"It's all you need."

He raises his eyes and I grin. "Many people here never lock their door. They have no need to. Crime is non-existent unless the odd apple goes missing from an overhanging tree."

"Now that is impressive."

He shakes his head. "I have a security system installed that rivals the Tower of London because burglary is rife where I live."

"I'm sorry to hear that."

"It's normal. Where I come from, that is."

"Well, that's another reason why you should make this your home."

He laughs out loud. "Don't hold back, Jessy. Tell me how it is."

Before I can reply, I notice one of the villagers heading our way and say quickly, "Okay, go along with this, and forget what I said about crime because there might be a murder in the next five minutes unless you follow my lead."

"What–"

I smile at Wilf as he approaches.

"Hey, Wilf, how's it going?"

"Oh, you know, Jessy, my bunions are playing up and I lost my dog again."

The shock on Luke's face makes me bite back my grin and I smile sympathetically. "She'll soon come back. She's probably taken off after a rabbit again."

"Then she better bring it back for tea. I've got nothing in."

Luke is staring uneasily at the shotgun that is slung over Wilf's shoulder as he turns to Luke and narrows his eyes.

"Who's the grockle?"

"Lady Townsend's nephew and the new owner of Granthaven."

Wilf leans forward and the stench of tobacco hangs heavy in the air.

"I had a lot of time for your aunt, son. She knew how to let her knickers down."

The shock on Luke's face is too funny and I say quickly, "Yes, she loved dancing and you probably meant letting her hair down, Wilf."

"I know what I meant."

He winks and this time I'm the one who is shocked and he peers at Luke a little closer. "I heard you're a footballer. What team?"

He narrows his eyes and before Luke can answer him, I say quickly, "Arsenal."

Luke makes to correct me, but Wilf slaps him on the back and then nods to his gun. "Bloody good job. I can't stand any other team and was likely to do you some damage if it was one of those northern ones."

Luke pales as I say with a slight cough.

"Yes, Wilf is Arsenal's biggest fan, aren't you, Wilf?"

"Sure am. Tell me, son, how is Dave?"

Luke's face is a picture and I prompt, "The goalkeeper, you know, David Seaman."

The fact he left years ago confuses Luke even further and Wilf chuckles. "I love good old Dave. Nothing gets past him. So, I bet you learned a lot from the master."

"Master?"

Luke is now losing the will to live as Wilf rolls his eyes. "Your manager who was named after the very club itself."

"Arsene." I add, hoping that Luke plays along and he nods slightly bemused. "Yes, he's an amazing man."

I clap my hands together and stamp my feet. "Anyway, we should go. Good luck finding Gripper, Wilf."

"Thanks, Jessy. Up the gunners." He says. lifting his gun in a salute and as he walks away, Luke gasps, "What the hell was that all about?"

I stare after Wilf and say sadly, "Alzheimers. It's getting worse. He lives in the past and his dog, Gripper, well she died twenty years ago. At the time Arsenal was run by Arsene Wenger and David Seaman was in the team back then. Wilf lives in that moment because it was his happiest time. He was also married to Betty, who died nine years ago, and it's as if his life ended with her."

"That's sad."

Luke stares after Wilf. "And they let him have a gun?"

The expression on his face makes me laugh. "A gun with no bullets. His neighbours Joe and Sadie look after him and make sure to remove anything he could use to cause himself, or anyone else harm. They cook his meals, wash his clothes, and he still believes Betty is responsible."

"That's sad."

"Not really. He's happy, for now, anyway."

I start walking because if Luke does sell up, Wilf is just one of the villagers who will be most affected by change. At the moment, he's happy and settled and living his best life. If he was forced to move or go into a home, it would probably finish him off.

CHAPTER 14
LUKE

There is a lot to think about and as we step over the wooden bridge and find the first cottage to our left, I say in a low voice, "Is this one of mine?"

I peer with dismay at the peeling paint on the windows and the thatch that is patchy at best, with plants growing through the cracks in the roof and Jessy nods.

"Yes. It's rented by a young couple who just got married. They don't have much and relied on wedding gifts and second hand finds to furnish the place."

I note the unkempt garden and peeling paint and my heart sinks. It appears gloomy due to the dark leaded windows and the surrounding trees and Jessy says brightly, "They are enthusiastic though and it will soon look amazing. I hope they stay, but from experience, young couples move on pretty quickly when they start a family because there is no school nearby that doesn't require a car journey and not much social life."

"I see."

To be honest, I don't blame them. *I* don't even want to live here and I own the bloody place. I picture my mansion back in Cheshire, along with the apartment I own in Manchester and it's a world away from where I am now.

We walk along a pretty lane with the stream running alongside us and I take a deep breath of pure clean air, something I never appreciated until now.

There are several cottages behind the stream on a bank that are pretty but obviously in need of some tender care, and Jessy waves in their direction.

"These are also yours. Most of the tenants have lived here for decades. They look after their gardens and in the summer you will see beautiful flowers and lines of washing blowing in the breeze."

"What do they do in winter?"

There is nothing here and Jessy shrugs. "Try to keep warm, cook, clean, work. The same as anyone else, really. We are part of civilisation too and are normal human beings who do what everybody else does."

"Of course. Forgive me."

I obviously touched a nerve because she is frowning and then we stop outside a house set at the junction where the road splits in two.

"This is our house."

She appears a little defensive and says awkwardly, "I don't suppose you'd mind if we stopped here for a minute. My parents must be home from Vienna, and I should reassure them that I'm safe."

"Of course."

I'm interested in seeing where Jessy lives and as we walk up the small stone path, she smiles apologetically as she opens the front door that is nestling underneath a large wooden porch.

"Jessy, is that you?"

A cheery voice calls out, and she shouts, "Yes, mum, but before you—"

A woman appears who looks a lot like her daughter and squeals as she rushes towards her and pulls her in for a hug.

"Darling, it's so good to be home."

She steps away and presses several kisses on Jessy's frozen cheeks, and then her gaze falls to me and her eyes open wide.

"Oh, I'm sorry."

"Mum, this is, um, Luke Adams, Lady Townsend's nephew. You know the–"

"Footballer."

She smiles widely. "Well, look at you. I heard you were visiting. This must have come as quite a shock to you."

"A little."

She nods toward the door she appeared out of. "Well, I'm Portia, named after the car but spelt differently and my husband is Terry, named after nothing in particular, but he's in the shower right now. Come in, I've just boiled the kettle and Jessy did a good job of lighting the fire, so the house is warm."

As we follow her into the kitchen, my first thought is how cosy it is. It's not the largest one I've ever seen, but it's the most welcoming one and the heat from the fire has warmed the room, making it the best place on earth right now.

"Take a seat, Luke. How do you like your coffee?"

"White, no sugar, thanks."

"So, how was Vienna?" Jessy asks with a smile.

Her mother nods, her eyes shining. "I still can't believe we were there. It was so magical. I was blown away by the spectacle and we even got to ride in one of those horse-drawn carriages around the city. You should go there, both of you."

Jessy's face flames and I can tell it's not from the warmth of the fire and I chuckle softly. "It sounds amazing."

"Have you ever been, Luke?" Portia asks, fixing me with an interested gleam in her eyes.

"No, but several of the guys visited in the past."

"You should go there. As I said, it was magical."

The door opens, and a man heads inside dressed in a warm sweater, his hair still damp from the shower.

"Terry, come and meet Luke, Lady Townsend's nephew."

"Oh yes."

He holds out his hand and shakes mine hard and says with a smile, "I'm pleased to meet you. I was sorry to hear about your aunt. We all loved her here."

I wish I could say the same, but I hardly knew her and it strikes me that I should be the one offering them my condolences, not the other way around.

It appears that we may be family, but your real family becomes the people who are involved in your life willingly. The fact I inherited her wealth isn't lost on me because I deserve none of it. If anything, the villagers do because they were here for her when I never gave her a second thought.

Images of her dancing with the locals, laughing and

sharing in their lives cross my mind and I wonder if anybody would be half as sad when I die. Sure, I may get a mention in the news, or perhaps I will have a family by then who will mourn my passing but right now there is only Steven, Morgana, a family I never see and a huge liability that goes by the name of Granthaven.

CHAPTER 15
JESSY

It's strange seeing Luke in my kitchen. Quite surreal really and as he chats to my parents, the scene almost appears normal. Then I picture his real life and the people he usually mixes with and my heart sinks.

He doesn't belong here. Not really. He may want to help, but he's got a life far from here and this must all seem dull in comparison to that.

Then there's Morgana.

The rather glamorous, attractive other half of him who *definitely* doesn't belong here. She will enjoy playing at renovation and acting a part but she will soon get bored. Granthaven is hardly the metropolis and definitely not a place for celebrities.

As soon as the excitement wears off, they will pack up and leave, and I should really let them get on with that.

As I peer into the window of a different world, it makes my own seem rather empty in comparison. Sure, I have family and friends, but I live their life, not my own. I am merely occupying space until I move on and forge my own family and I hate the fact it will more than likely not be here.

The young couple who have just moved into Stream View probably won't hang around either. As soon as they have enough money, they will take advantage of a shared ownership property in Dorchester, or scrape enough together to rent a house in a better location. Granthaven has always been a stop gap due to its cheap rents and no rules and I must admit that's all it's good for now.

I tune back into their conversation and wish I had kept listening as Luke exclaims, "The night the mistletoe died?"

"Yes, Luke. It's a tradition in Granthaven. It's staged every year."

His gaze rests on my heated face and I say quickly, "Luke doesn't want to hear about that, mum. Anyway, tell me about Vienna. What was your hotel like?"

Luke holds up his hand.

"No, I'm interested. Tell me."

I glare at mum as she sits in the kitchen chair, her hand wrapped around a mug of coffee and says with a deep breath, "I'll tell you the story behind the tradition if you like."

I make to protest and Luke says quickly. "Please. I'm interested."

She smiles as she begins the story I have grown up listening to and is woven into the fabric of life in Granthaven.

"Many years ago Granthaven was a thriving community presided over by Lord and Lady Townsend. Life was good, and it was a happy time and the gracious landowners involved the village in every aspect of their lives. Christmas was a partic-

ular favourite of the Townsends because it was the perfect excuse to throw many parties, the entire village pulling together to make a happy time. They used holly with berries and ivy to decorate the manor house. They were tied into glorious swags around every surface, along with bunches of mistletoe hanging all around. Candles burned on mantles and the fires roared in the grates and the mistletoe was in abundance due to the lady of the house's love of the plant. She loved how it reminded her of happy times and the magic that comes from togetherness, kindness, and the spirit of Christmas. When the entire village came together to celebrate happy times and it became an important addition to the festivities. It was tradition that a woman caught under the mistletoe had to return any kiss offered or not receive any marriage proposals for a year. Back then, it was the most important thing in a woman's life to secure a good marriage, so the threat was a very real one. A few years later Lady Townsend grew sick. The lord was extremely worried about her and engaged the most eminent doctors to cure her. It was to no avail, and she died on Christmas Eve. The very night she loved above all others. It was the darkest time in Granthaven's history and when the lord woke on Christmas Day, it was to the devastating sight that all the mistletoe had died. All around the house were shrivelled bunches of the sacred plant and the lord, in his grief, scoured the land to replace it, discovering every bunch in the trees had also died. To this day, not one sprig of mistletoe has ever grown in Granthaven and legend has it that when the heart has been restored to the village, the mistletoe will grow again."

Mum smiles softly. "So, every year the villagers stage a pantomime celebrating the legend so that even if the mistletoe has died, the meaning behind it lives on."

"The meaning?" Luke asks, obviously riveted by the story and mum nods.

"Yes, when the manor is filled with true love and happiness, the mistletoe will thrive and all it takes is one kiss under its bough to restore the estate to its former glory."

She points to me and I want the ground to swallow me up.

"Jessy is playing Lady Townsend this year and Scott Barnes has been roped in to play the lord. It was Grace's turn this year, but she's off on her travels, so Jessy had to step up."

"Scott Barnes?" Luke leans forward.

I add, "My friend's brother, which is a huge problem."

"Why?"

I pull a face. "Because Scott is like my older brother and the thought of kissing him screams incest, and I am still working out a way to change the script."

"Good luck with that, darling. It's the entire point of the play." Mum rolls her eyes and I sigh heavily.

"Anyway, we should continue our tour of the village. We only stopped to say hi, oh and to tell you I've got a job."

"Oh my God!"

Mum jumps up and dad says loudly, "Congratulations my clever girl."

"It's not in London, is it?" Mum's face falls and dad slips his arm around her shoulder and squeezes her in a show of support.

"No, it's um, working for Luke, actually."

"I don't understand."

Mum peers between us and Luke nods. "I heard of

Jessy's degree and I'm looking for a business manager to help me with Granthaven, and she was the perfect fit."

"That's amazing news. Oh my God."

Mum tears away from dad and hugs Luke hard, who appears a little bewildered and dad claps him on the back and shakes his free hand vigorously as mum clings onto him like a limpet on coral.

"Thank you so much. That's such good news. We should crack open the elderflower wine to celebrate."

"NO!" I say in horror as dad sprints over to the larder cupboard.

"Nonsense, Jessy, this is the perfect time to uncork the vintage elderflower." Mum adds, and I stand, holding my hands out in front of me. "No. Please."

Suddenly, it's as if one of Wilf''s guns has gone off as the cork explodes from its tether and sprays elderflower wine all over the room, causing my parents to yell with delight as dad grabs a glass and yells, "Don't waste it. It's good stuff."

He hands the glass to a bemused-looking Luke and as they hand one to me and fill their own glasses, dad says loudly, "To a long and happy partnership."

Luke catches my eye and grins and I have never downed a glass of my dad's elderflower wine as fast as this one because what the hell is happening to me? I am falling hard for another woman's man and, to make matters worse, he is paying me for the privilege.

CHAPTER 16
LUKE

I wonder if it's possible to fall in love with a place at first sight. People at first sight even, because the more I see of Granthaven and its inhabitants, the more I like.

This is a drastic change from my usual surroundings. I don't see anyone where I live. I head into my car, parked behind the security gates at home or the training ground, and drive between them. It's like I'm stuck on a tightrope, only going back and forth between two places. During away games, the coach becomes my security guard, while my teammates act as a shield against everyday life.

This is life.

Raw, real, desperate but wonderful life. The people here have hardly anything, materialistically speaking, but they are richer than me because they have a soul.

As I watch Jessy with her parents, it reminds me of my own rather hollow life. I visit my parents but they are too busy travelling to make elderflower wine and partake in village life.

Then there's me.

I've never even met my neighbours, let alone care for them and it started to hit home as we walked around the village – slowly, due to my freaking boot – giving Jessy ample time to describe the lives of the inhabitants of the cottages we passed.

They had one thing mainly in common and that was the number of years they have lived here. It appears that the majority stay and make it their home, although I detected the sadness in Jessy's voice when she spoke of the future.

If anything, I feel terrible as we complete the tour and I've witnessed firsthand the decay of a once thriving village and my heart sinks at the mammoth task stretching before me like an impossible dream.

I'm already aware this won't work. I'm not the saviour of the village – far from it. As much as I want to help, I'm just not rich enough, or clever enough to make the villager's dreams come true and yet the animation in Jessy's expression as she speaks of her home, tugs on my heartstrings and gives me the determination to try.

∼

I LEAVE Jessy to head home and I try to shake away the disappointment I'm experiencing inside when she walks away from me.

I wonder why I like her so much. I meet many women but most of them are above reality. They live a pampered life, living it more through their social media than anything else, and yet Jessy's life is very real indeed.

As soon as I head back inside, Morgana greets me with a worried frown.

"Oh, Luke, thank goodness you're back."

"Why, what's happened?"

I shrug out of my coat because hallelujah, Jasper's storage heaters appear to be working well and the place doesn't freeze my breath like it did before.

"The production team won't make it here for another day at least, and Jasper is desperate to begin. He wants us to film a few candid shots and do some interviews for the camera about our first impressions of this place. You know the kind of thing they do on the series I watch."

I groan inside because this is Morgana's thing and not mine, and I still can't believe I agreed to this at all.

"Please, Luke. For me."

Her eyes are wide and hopeful, and it strikes me how pretty she looks. She is made up perfectly for the camera and is wearing a cashmere red sweater with white jeans and fur boots.

Morgana is an extremely attractive woman and deserves the adulation of her followers. She is funny, self deprecating and loves to offer tips and discount codes for the products she endorses. She is also working on her own beauty line and I'm sure Jessy would be fascinated by the business she is creating in cyberspace. Many people underestimate Morgana, but that person was never me.

"Okay babe. What do you want me to do?"

Her brilliant smile is edged in relief and she presses a light kiss to my lips and whispers, "Thanks, hun. I know you hate this kind of thing, but it really helps."

I roll my eyes. "Just tell me what to do."

. . .

BEFORE I KNOW what's happening, we are sitting side by side on the couch by the roaring fire, Morgana's hand resting on my knee and my arm slung around her shoulder. The very picture of domestic bliss and loves young dream.

Jasper is filming the segment and asks the questions that we dutifully answer in a tried and tested reality format.

"What are your first impressions of Granthaven, Luke? It must be a world away from Manchester and the life of a premier league footballer."

"It certainly is."

I smile into the camera. "I'm pleasantly surprised, though it does require a lot of work."

"A lot." Morgana interrupts, rolling her eyes and she adds, "We look on it as a challenge, don't we, darling?"

Before I can answer, she gazes at the camera with a dreamy expression. "I must confess I love it, though. I mean, it's so Pride and Prejudice. Who wouldn't love being part of history and being surrounded by a place that it appears time forgot? We are blown away, aren't we, darling?"

"We are." I gaze at her fondly as she laughs softly.

"We have so many plans for the restoration. Luke has even appointed a local business manager to help us. Isn't that right, darling?"

"Yes, she will be invaluable."

"You see–" Morgana smiles into the camera. "We have a real chance to make a difference and don't take that responsibility lightly. Luke was left with this amazing legacy and we must make it work for everyone's sakes."

I nod, a little uneasy because now there's even more pressure because if we fail, it will be all over the internet and for a man who likes to win, this is a challenge I must give my best shot.

CHAPTER 17
JESSY

I swear I am permanently cold and tonight is no exception. I tug my padded coat a little tighter around me and wish I hadn't ever agreed to this stupid pantomime. Angie stepped up last year and her lord was Edward Cummins, the rather lecherous son of Sandra and Neil Cummins, who have lived in the village for ten years already.

"So, how did it go?" Angie asks as we huddle under a blanket while we wait for our lines and I whisper, "Surprising."

"In a good way?"

"Yes."

I hate that I'm smiling and I hate the knowing glint in her eye even more as she whispers, "You like him, don't you?"

"NO!" I yell, causing a few raised eyebrows in our direction and I lower my voice, "I mean, yes, I do like him in a friendship sort of way, but not like you're thinking."

"Are you sure about that?" Her impish smile makes me laugh and then I sigh.

"If he wasn't already attached to the sweetest, most glamorous woman, then I suppose he is attractive. However, he's already taken, so I have no right being attracted to him. It's purely business, nothing else."

"My darling, the villagers are here. Come and welcome them with me."

I glance up, the familiar line my cue to join them and I yell, *"I am so excited. Christmas Eve is my most favourite day of the year. Come, we shall greet them together."*

I remain seated because this is merely a read through and Scott looks as interested in the proceedings as I am.

"Lady Townsend, the first guests, have arrived."

Angie says and Scott continues, *"You look amazing, my dear, and the house is a triumph."*

He pauses and then says with a sigh, *"We appear to be standing under the mistletoe. Can you spare a kiss for the man who loves you more than Christmas itself?"*

I take a breath because whoever wrote this script should be fired. It's so incredibly cringe.

"Mistletoe, my favourite Christmas tradition. I wonder if any of the maidens from the parish will benefit from its magic this evening?"

"There is only one fair lady I'm interested in and I'm looking at her."

Scott pretends to gag and I flip him off as I say with a giggle, *"Oh, Barnaby, I can never resist you."*

Angie nudges me and I note the stricken expression in her brother's eye as he attempts to say the words none of us ever want to say out loud. Our script reading is suddenly interrupted when a side door opens and an icy blast causes us to shiver under the blankets as it fills the small hall.

I gaze in surprise as Luke and Morgana enter, closely followed by the man with the camera and Mr Spalding jumps up and almost falls over himself as he rushes to greet them.

"Mr Adams and Miss–"

"Morgana, please." She says, pulling her fur coat a little tighter around her as she visibly shivers.

"How may I help you?"

Mr Spalding is tripping over his words in his haste and the chill inside me is instantly chased away as Luke catches my eye and grins. It's as if we are the only ones in the room as the moment suspends in time and then Morgana interrupts the silence and says loudly, "Luke told me about the pantomime and the rehearsal and we were so hoping to offer our services."

Scott looks at Luke hopefully and my heart beats a little faster as Luke nods. "Please, let us help in a small way, the first thing being to offer you a room at the house to rehearse in. It's much warmer than here and way too big for us alone."

Mr Spalding looks as if he is about to drop to his knees in a reverent bow and Mrs Jameson says quickly, "Well, if you're sure, it is a little cold in here."

Before Luke can even reply, the villagers are rushing to gather their things and heading for the door before he can draw breath and Angie nudges me and whispers, "Wow, I wouldn't miss this for the world."

We gather our own things and follow the stampeding

crowd as they follow Luke and Morgana like the Pied Piper.

"She is gorgeous." Angie sighs beside me and I have to agree.

"She is."

"I wouldn't say no," Scott adds as he falls into step beside us and Angie replies, "That's your trouble, you never do."

I giggle because Scott is a terrible flirt and chats to many girls on his phone, never settling on one in particular, and he gives the term playing the field a new meaning entirely. He is a serial flirt and believes one woman will never be enough, much to the disgust of his parents, who firmly believe in one at a time.

"I can't wait to see what they've done with the house." Angie adds, and I shake my head.

"They've only just arrived. Give them a chance."

It doesn't take long for us to reach the manor house and I'm conscious the man with the camera is recording every step we take and as we head through the large oak wooden front door, I stare around in surprise at the transformation.

Somehow, they have made this place feel warm and there are even some large arrangements with foliage from the garden in huge vases.

"It's a bit different from yesterday." Angie says in awe as she glances around, as if seeing the place in a new light.

"We can use the formal sitting room." Morgana calls, "There is a fire going, and I made some mulled wine."

Even I am now in love with Morgana and as we troop into the sitting room, I no longer see the tired threadbare furniture because with just a bit of kindness, they have made the formerly austere room a welcoming space that is suddenly filled with lighthearted chatter.

CHAPTER 18
LUKE

This was Morgana's idea, and is one of her better ones. It feels good helping the villagers. Apparently, a warm fire, and some mulled wine go a long way to paste a smile on their faces.

As they shrug out of their coats and Morgana hands around the glasses of steaming nectar, I sneak a glance at Jessy who is chatting to another young woman. I could stare at Jessy all night because her cheeks are now rosy with the effects of the heat and alcohol and her eyes sparkle against the flames of the fire. Her soft lips are curled in a smile as she chats with her friend.

I note the young man sitting with them and guess it's her friend's brother and the fact he's tapping away on his phone tells me he is here under duress.

"Jolly nice of you, Mr Adams."

The older man says by my side and I turn my attention reluctantly to him instead.

"It's the least we could do."

I don't mention that Jasper thought it was the perfect

event to get involved with and has planned out every detail already, from the performance being acted in this very house, to reenact the legend in situ.

This is a conniving plan for airtime in the national press and he intends on securing sponsorship by shining the spotlight on our plans to make Granthaven profitable again. If we fail, nobody could blame us for not trying and as I note Jessy's soft laughter floating across the room in my direction, right now, in this moment, I will do whatever it takes to keep it there.

"So, don't let us interrupt, carry on as you were," Morgana says and pats the seat beside her on one of the settees. "Sit with me darling. This will be such fun."

I head over to her side with an easy grin and as we sit snuggled up together, I watch with interest as the villagers carry on where they left off.

"Um–" Scott appears a little tongue tied and Mr Spalding says loudly, "The line was – we appear to be standing under the mistletoe. Can you spare a kiss for the man who loves you more than Christmas itself?"

I want to laugh out loud, and then the soft pitch of Jessy's voice turns my attention to her.

"Oh, Barnaby, I thought you'd never ask."

Morgana gets a fit of the giggles and I nudge her, causing her to cough and she says apologetically, "Sorry guys, the wine went down the wrong way. Please, carry on."

Jessy's face must be as red as the burning ash in the fire as she catches my eye, and I raise my glass and grin, causing her to roll her eyes as Scott says in a pained voice, *"You taste of Christmas my darling. Happiness, and cinnamon spice."*

Jasper lowers his camera and shakes his head, apparently shocked, and says loudly, "Excuse me, but um, cut."

Everyone looks in his direction as he throws his hands up in the air. "This will never do. Where did you get this script from?"

Mr Spalding says quickly, "My wife, Alana. She's an aspiring screen writer and has given us the copywrite to use her masterpiece."

I catch Jessy's eye and she grins before pretending to stick a knife in her heart.

Jasper shakes his head. "Well, it won't do. If we are going to televise this in the show, it must be more in keeping with today's standards. If I may suggest, I'll send it to my production company to modernise. It will set us back a week or so, but I believe will work a miracle in the long run."

I quickly interject because Mr Spalding appears to be about to have a coronary. "Obviously it's an amazing script, very applicable to Granthaven and perhaps what Jasper means is it could use a little enhancement to align with the television companies' standards of practice. It will be done for legal reasons, nothing else."

I throw Jasper a warning glare and he nods. "Yes, that's what I meant."

Mr Spalding sighs heavily. "In that case, I have no objection, but what is this about televising it?"

Scott looks up in horror as Jessy turns extremely pale and Jasper shrugs. "We thought it would be an amazing addition to the reality tv show. Obviously, the performance will be restricted to a few scenes, but the rehearsals and subsequent success will be documented as another example of why Granthaven is special."

I must admit that Jasper knows how to win over a crowd because the murmurs of excitement coming from the villagers, assures me of their cooperation. All except Scott and Jessy, who are staring at one another in horror.

Morgana whispers, "Pray to God Jasper works a miracle on that script or those poor actors will be the laughingstock of Christmas. Honestly, this script is a disgrace. I feel bad for them."

As the villagers chat amongst themselves, Morgana says softly, "We should mingle. It will be good for morale and demonstrate we are fitting in."

Before I can respond, she heads to a small group and I notice their smiles grow a little wider as they gaze at her with adoration.

I note Mr Spalding heading my way and quickly move in the opposite direction towards Jessy and her friend, and as I drop into the couch beside them, her friend says reverently, "This is so good of you."

"I suppose." I feel bad because it certainly wasn't done out of kindness, just money and exposure, and Jessy nods. "It is, but I'm not happy about being on national television in a play that will make me a laughingstock."

She appears so forlorn, I want to reassure her and say with a smile. "It will be fine. Jasper will work it out. It's his profession, and he's good at it."

"Forgive me for asking, Luke–" Her friend interrupts. "How is your profession?"

"Angie!" Jessy gasps and I shrug.

"It's fine."

I nod at my boot.

"This comes off next week and then I begin physio."

"You're leaving?" Angie's face falls.

"No, the club is sending one of our physios here. He arrives next week and we will work on restoring my ankle to its former glory."

"That's very generous of them." Angie grins. "I mean, my uncle Jim had a fall last month, and he's still on the waiting list at Dorchester hospital. It pays to have friends in high places, I'm guessing."

I know she didn't mean to make me feel bad, but I do. It only illustrates how much I have in comparison to them and it's all because of business. The club pays me a fortune to perform and all the time I'm injured I'm not generating the money they pay me for.

"It does, but only because I'm a liability."

"How?" she adds with curiosity as she leans forward, intent on my answer.

"I'm a commodity to them. It's not because they are concerned about my health or wellbeing. It's because they are paying me a huge salary to play football. All the time I'm injured they aren't getting their money's worth and if I'm broken beyond repair, they will replace me with a younger, more intact model."

"That's harsh." She says with anger and Jessy nods, her own expression mirroring that of her friend.

"It's the way it works." Scott speaks up.

"How do you know? You've never been out of Dorset?" Angie reprimands him and Scott shrugs.

"I have been all over the world because I have the internet. You don't have to travel to understand how the world works these days."

I laugh out loud at the expressions on the girl's faces and we are interrupted as Mr Spalding drops down before me on his knees and says apologetically. "I'm sorry to interrupt but, I, well, it's just–"

I smile my encouragement, and he exhales sharply. "The script. My *wife's* script. I hope she will still be credited as the author."

"Of course."

He breathes a little easier. "Good. Perhaps there may even be a little renumeration fee; a royalty perhaps for the movie rights?"

Jessy and Angie stare at him in shock as he stutters, "I mean, we don't want to be exploited and, well, she may become famous and her words have value."

The girl's eyes turn to me and I say carefully, "I can't promise anything, but I'll mention it to Jasper. He will know more about it than me."

He nods and stands, glancing at his wristwatch.

"Well, if that's all for tonight, I must dash because Alana has a knitting club in the next village and requires a lift home. I hope you don't mind me broaching the subject, but as her business manager, it is a pertinent question that I must ask."

He moves swiftly away and Angie says in a low voice, "Bloody cheek. She's lucky we're even agreeing to act her horrendous script, let alone demand payment for it."

Jessy laughs and says with an amused twinkle in her eye. "I must say I'm impressed. I never knew he had it in him and why not see if he can earn something from it?"

"I agree with Jessy." I offer her a warm smile and then glance up as Steven drops beside me and whispers, "The guvnor wants a word."

My heart falls because if the manager of Manchester Rangers is calling me, it must be important.

"I'm sorry. I need to take this call. Please, stay as long as you want."

I note several of the cast packing up and am surprised how much I want Jessy and her friend to stay. They smile, but as I walk away, I'm guessing they will be long gone when I finish my call.

CHAPTER 19
JESSY

We watch Luke leave and Angie sighs wistfully. "Wow, he's gorgeous."

"He is."

We stare after him like lovesick puppies and then straighten up as his girlfriend heads our way.

She takes his vacated seat and grins. "Wow, I don't know how you managed to keep a straight face. That script is hideous."

Angie laughs out loud. "You've got that right. It's no better than the one we acted last year when I had the misfortune to play Lady Townsend. It was far more serious and rather blood thirsty and ended up with me vomiting fake blood and staggering to my death like Lady Macbeth."

Morgana laughs and the twinkle in her eyes is friendly as she says with interest.

"So, I've met Jessy and know exactly what she now does for a living, but what about you, hun?"

Angie smiles. "I'm training to be a beauty therapist and also work at The Pigeon Trail to earn money."

"What's that?"

Morgana's eyes widen and I say quickly, "The local pub, just outside Granthaven. Despite the name, it's a cosy place to be and has an amazing inglenook fireplace that we are grateful for."

Morgana leans forward with interest.

"A beauty therapist. Do you do private work?"

"I do. What did you have in mind?"

Angie is serious now that she's wearing her business hat and Morgana studies her perfect nails and sighs. "I like to have my nails done every three days. I mean, I could do it myself, but it's never the same. I don't suppose you could help me out with that?"

Angie's eyes light up. "I would be honoured."

"I'll pay the going rate, of course."

"I, um–"

Angie falters and I can tell she's embarrassed to state a figure and I note the understanding in Morgana's eyes as she says briskly, "I usually pay fifty pounds for a manicure. Is that okay with you? I can pay cash or via bank transfer weekly of one hundred and fifty pounds."

Angie appears to have lost the power of speech and merely nods as Morgana points to Jasper. "He may need to film us occasionally and you might be asked a few questions about village life. Is that okay with you, or would you prefer extra money for stage fees?"

"No."

Angie shakes her head quickly. "The money is more than enough and I would be honoured to help out with your show."

Her eyes are shining, which causes me to smile. I love how happy Angie is to be working with her idol. I wonder if Morgana realises that Angie spends hours watching her videos and copying her style. This is a dream come true for my friend and I'm happy that Morgana is as nice as she appears to be in her videos. If anything, it leaves a Morgana sized hole in my heart because I like her almost as much as I do her boyfriend and I must remind myself that I'm here on business and that is all they require from me.

∽

Luke never came back and as we walk home, Scott having left an hour ago, Angie links her arm in mine and whispers, "We are so lucky they came here."

"We are." I must admit and she sighs, the moon peeking through the clouds, casting the countryside in a ghostly light, the odd sound from a night owl reminding us that the night belongs to him now.

"Do you think they'll stay?" She asks, and I hate the way my heart sinks.

"No. I don't." I sigh heavily, my breath dancing as a cloud in the icy air.

"They have a very different life than the one on offer here. They're young, with the world at their feet. Why would they bury themselves here in the countryside? It's sad but inevitable."

"I'm sure you're right, but they're here now."

Angie grips my arm a little tighter and her soft laugh carries on the slight breeze.

"Perhaps Granthaven will weave its magic around

their heart and they will decide life here is worth more than one where they live in mansions and drive fast flash cars, accepting invitations to film premieres and eating at exclusive restaurants."

I add. "Exactly. I mean, they would be fools not to trade that all in for nights spent plugging holes where the leaks find a way in and stamping the mud off their boots when they take the rubbish out."

"Obviously, they would hate to miss the annual harvest supper at the Spaldings and the village fete that involves Wilf shooting at tin cans and organising the dog and ferret run."

"Who needs celebrity parties and designer shopping sprees, luxury holidays in exotic places and designers lining up with gifts in the hope you wear their creations and spark sales?"

"I would hate that, wouldn't you, Jessy?" Angie groans. "Imagine not helping dredge the stream of sticks that have fallen in from the apple tree and being stung by wasps when you attempt to pick the plums from the orchard."

"Yes, fruit harvesting day would be so much more pleasurable and exciting than any guest appearance on a talk show or VIP visit to watch a football game."

We reach my house first and I stamp the ice forming on my feet. "Are you coming in for some hot chocolate?"

"I thought you'd never ask."

WE HEAD inside the dimly lit hallway, courtesy of the candles burning on the side and the dull flicker of the bulb in the faded lamp on the table.

We shrug out of our coats and mum calls out, "Is that you, Jessy?"

"Yes, Angie too."

"Come in love. We're just flicking through the photos from our trip."

I mouth, 'sorry' to Angie and we head inside the brightly lit kitchen where there are Christmas carols playing on the radio and the scent of hot chocolate and cookies greets us.

"We had such fun in Vienna, Angie. Come and see the ones where we took the horse-drawn carriage around the city."

We settle down to flick through mum's phone as she makes some drinks and dad grumbles, "It was bloody cold though. Even colder than Granthaven."

"But that was festive, right?" I say pointedly and mum moans.

"You'll never change your dad, love. He's always moaning about something. He thrives on misery."

Angie grins and then says with excitement. "You'll never guess what happened at rehearsals."

As she fills them in, my thoughts turn to Luke and Morgana and for some reason, I google them on my phone. Many images show up of them at various red carpet events and laughing into the camera, his arm slung affectionately around her shoulders.

It doesn't make me feel any better because they make such a great couple and I know they are nice with it. They really do have everything it seems and I wonder if this job was such a great idea after all.

I glance around the familiar kitchen, listening to the happy chatter and feel bad that I'm even resenting my life a little. The trouble is, I want more. I always have, which is why I went to university. Coming home has only reinforced that, and then Luke and Morgana arrived. Suddenly, I am yearning for something so far out of reach I would need a rocket ship to reach it. Their world isn't *my* world and I hate that more than anything, I wish that it was.

CHAPTER 20
LUKE

Steven is regarding me with a serious expression, and I sigh.

"He wants a daily progress report. The schedule is jam-packed over the Christmas period and he's conscious some of the players will need resting after the event. He told me he can't afford to be without me for long and a broken ankle isn't the end of the world."

"To him maybe, but it could be to you if it doesn't heal properly."

Steven rakes his fingers through his hair and exhales sharply. "I'll try to sort it. Just concentrate on your recovery and leave the business side to me. It's what you pay me for, after all."

I nod, but my heart is heavy as real life interferes with my new one.

"What are you going to do about the tax bill for the inheritance?"

Steven reminds me the government wants their pound of flesh and even though my aunt had several share accounts and savings that made my eyes water, we are still short of several millions of pounds.

"I don't know."

My face must fall because he smiles. "Perhaps Jessy will have a few ideas on how to raise some money. She seems keen. Perhaps she's just what you need right now."

"Perhaps."

I don't say much, but Steven isn't stupid and will be wondering why she is suddenly the most important person in my life. I'm not even sure myself and I stare out of the window and note how tranquil this place is. If anything, I envy the villagers because they enjoy a simple life. They may be suffering with cold homes and disrepair, but it is still somebody else's problem.

"You could sell some of the properties I guess." Steven remarks, trying to be of some help and I sigh.

"I can't. It's all tied up in the estate and whoever did it knew their stuff because I can't sell a field without going against some clause or another. Granthaven is Granthaven in the entirety, or not at all."

STEVEN HEADS off to do whatever Steven does, leaving me with more problems than I can carry on my already burdened shoulders. I glance at the boot on my foot and wonder what's happening underneath it.

Football has always been the most important thing in my life from a very early age. My father always encouraged me to follow my dreams and I picture my parents far away in their villa in Florida and wonder what they would think of Jessy. It shocks me that I'm thinking of her at all because I am Luke Adams.

Premier league hotshot, soon to be engaged to the gorgeous influencer, Morgana. Women like Jessy don't feature in my life at all, but in another life, one when I'm not any of those things, she is the kind of woman I could see myself settling down with. Pretty, clever, kind and sweet. The perfect wife, the perfect woman – for me, anyway.

I'm guessing she will marry a man who fits in with her way of life. They will work hard and have a family, filling their home with happiness and laughter. A simple life, one out of the spotlight. A life that is strangely appealing and one without millions of debt and hundreds, if not thousands, of people watching their every move and commenting on it.

"Hey."

I glance up and Morgana smiles as she sets a mug of coffee before me on the battered wooden desk.

"You are deep in thought."

"I am."

I smile as she takes the seat opposite and leans on her elbows, her pretty face gazing at me with a hint of worry.

"Is it your leg?"

"Partly."

She smiles reassuringly. "It will be fine, hun. Ankles heal and yours will be no exception."

"You're probably right."

"Anyway–" Her eyes sparkle as she arrives at the real reason she's here.

"Jasper tells me the production crew will arrive tomorrow. I've made up the beds with fresh linen this time and Mrs Sims – Karen – was a great help. When the crew arrives, most will be staying in their motorhome that we have decided to set up in the field behind the cricket pitch and filming will start the following day."

"It sounds as if you have it all worked out."

"I always do."

She gazes at me with a thoughtful expression.

"Just say if you're not okay with this."

"Really?" I raise my eyes, knowing that if I did voice any concerns, Morgana would be crushed. This is what she lives for, thrives on, and my cooperation is the most important thing to her.

"I know I don't say this often, Luke."

I glance up in surprise as she says softly, "But I do love you."

"I love you too."

I smile, my gaze softening because I do love Morgana. With my entire heart. We are good together, work well together and, more importantly, are friends. Our lives are intertwined and most of the time I'm happy about that, but then a pretty face turned my head with sparkling blue eyes and a vulnerable edge that brought out the protector in me.

A woman I would never have met had it not been for my aunt and yet now I have, despite the mess my life is currently in, I can think of nothing else but working out ways to spend time in her company.

Morgana leaves me to my thoughts and heads off to do what she does best and as the door closes behind her, I stare out of the window at the peaceful view.

Tomorrow it will change when this world collides with my new one and Granthaven will be thrust onto the world stage. There will be nowhere left to hide and tonight is like Christmas Eve before Santa comes and

Christmas chaos dances around our hearts like a lit firework.

The calm before the storm rages, and all the preparations come to fruition. The moment before a game where we all wait in the tunnel, praying that everything turns out the way we planned.

The night before everything changes.

The night before the mistletoe died.

CHAPTER 21
JESSY

I never imagined my first day at work would be this one. As I sit before Luke in his decaying study, I am more nervous than I've ever been. This is a big deal for me. The chance to prove myself and make a difference and, more than anything, I don't want to let him down.

He is already so kind and yet I detect a hint of worry in his smile and note the tired shadows under his eyes, and I'm guessing he has a lot on his mind right now.

He sighs and gazes out of the window and I note the pattern of ice forming in intricate patterns over the glass and the frosted bushes outside. The sun is shining though, and it's a glorious winter's day, but from the atmosphere inside this room, there is a dark cloud looming.

"So, Jessy." He turns back to me and smiles. "Tell me how to raise millions of pounds to pay off the tax man and restore Granthaven to its former glory, hopefully before my ankle heals and the new year dawns."

He makes light of the situation, but I'm aware his words are edged in truth and I remove my notebook from my bag and open it to the page I scribbled down some ideas a long time ago.

"I've had some thoughts, but you may not agree with them."

"Hit me with them."

He smiles and leans forward and I note how his dark brown eyes are like soft velvet pools of the richest chocolate and I shift on my seat and attempt to drag my mind into business.

"The first thing to do is make a list of your assets and income streams."

I chew on the end of my pen as I stare down at my notes.

"I did some research and there is the rental from the properties, of course. You could raise the rent a little, but the repairs needed wouldn't justify that until they are dealt with."

He leans back and sighs. "Go on."

"There is a working farm under an assured tenancy and the well-established woodland provides the opportunity to develop the excellent pheasant and partridge shoot, accessed by a series of conveniently laid out tracks. There is also a managed deer population managed by the Game keeper and the Valley of Stones located within the estate is a National Nature Reserve."

I glance up and smile reassuringly. "They are all thriving and managed well but could be developed into thriving businesses, encouraging corporate breaks and potentially team building events that command a hefty fee. I suggest arranging a meeting with the company who are currently managing the estate as they will have more insight into that than I can offer."

"I have that on my list. A man called Geoffrey Knight handles it. Do you know him?"

I nod. "I've seen him around the village, but he doesn't come here much and when he did, it was mainly to the house to see Lady Townsend."

I peer at my notes.

"In total, there are thirty-two properties which are mainly located within the village, with six in off-lying farm or woodland settings. The majority are let on assured short-hold tenancies. As I mentioned, they are a good source of revenue and there are several dilapidated barns and unused houses that with renovation may bring in more revenue."

"That would cost money I don't have."

I hate how defeated he looks already and smile my encouragement.

"The majority of the land is classified as grade three on the agricultural land classification, meaning it's suitable for all cereals, legumes and grassland. It has been a dairy farm for a number of years but I'm guessing you could diversify and incorporate food production into your operation and potentially convert one of the outbuildings into a farm shop, possibly a children's farm to encourage tourism and school trips to name just a couple of opportunities."

"That will cost more money to set up."

He leans back and rakes his fingers through his hair and I wish it was possible to wave a magic wand and make all his problems disappear. With an encouraging smile, I continue.

"The majority of land is grassland that could be utilised in another way, possibly camping, but that would require a few amenities such as showers, toilets, waste disposal, that kind of thing."

"That would take more money to set up."

He shakes his head and I sense my plans slipping away as he bolts back to Manchester and I take a deep breath.

"The woodlands are under forest management and provide an excellent source of timber that supplies many of the timber yards around here. You may possibly set up one yourself and offset the costs by selling it to trade as well as the chippings for gardens as mulch."

He smiles, and I am fixated on the twinkle in his eyes as he says with a smile, "You've done your homework."

"I told you. I used Granthaven as the basis for my thesis and I got a first."

I am so proud of that, and he nods his appreciation. "I'm impressed and can see why."

I take a deep breath. "Then there are the village hall and the church. They are perfect for functions and weddings, bringing me back to the house itself."

I glance around the ancient room and note the faded furnishings and peeling paper and my heart sinks, but I push it aside and say with enthusiasm.

"There are ten bedrooms and many other reception rooms, including a library, a swimming pool, billiards room and prayer room, although I'm guessing that would be better used as another reception room."

I tap my pen on my book and smile. "There is a tennis court in fairly good condition and extensive gardens. Although mainly set to lawn for ease of upkeep. Obviously, there is the lake and down the lane is the walled garden which is a great source of food for the entire village with a tea room set just outside it. Once again, these businesses could be developed along with the orchard that has an abundance of fruit trees where Maisy Miggins makes preserves from the fruit and Jasper Cole uses the apples to make cider."

"Villagers, I take it." He asks and I nod.

"Yes, Lady Townsend was happy for them to do it in exchange for a supply of their products. That's what village life is like here in Granthaven. We help one another and expect nothing but goodwill in return."

"Which is half your problem."

Luke sighs heavily. "From what I can tell, this has all the makings of a profitable enterprise but would take millions to make happen. What are your thoughts on raising the capital?"

I shift on my seat and turn the page in my notebook.

"Aside from your current income, I would turn my attention to anything of value not tied up in the legacy."

"Such as?"

My heart sinks. "Well, I'm guessing there are several valuable commodities inside the house itself. Paintings, antiques, a prizewinning cellar that Lord Townsend was particularly proud of, to name but a few things."

"I guess, but those things hardly bring in millions."

I fix him with an exasperated look.

"Listen, Luke, nobody said this would be easy and yes, this requires an outside investment. I am merely telling you what's on offer. Now you need to form a business plan and pitch it for investment. There are so many plus points and very few minus ones, but it requires a cash injection to get started. All businesses incur start-up costs and so you must work out how to pitch your investment and watch the money flooding in. I mean –"

I'm anxious knowing I must pitch this right if I'm to capture his interest in the project.

"The reality show is the perfect opportunity. Use it to present your business to the world. Who knows who will see it and fall in love with the dream? Set up a management company, offer shares in it, sell the dream and it may become a reality. I have every faith in you."

I lean forward and say with enthusiasm, "Both you and Morgana are in the perfect position to drum up interest. Use your platforms to appeal to the followers. Morgana might run yoga retreats in yurts in the grounds. I've heard there is big money in that. Glamping in the forest and lodges brings in money. The opportunities are endless if you apply vision."

Luke nods and a slow smile spreads across his face and he says in his husky voice, "I admire your enthusiasm, Jessy and you have definitely sold the dream. Perhaps the first step would be to arrange a meeting with Geoffrey Knight and see where we go from there."

I sigh with relief and lean back in my chair, my heart racing as I attempt to get it under control.

Luke makes a few notes and then smiles, the atmosphere changing in a heartbeat from business to pleasure as he says lightly, "I don't know about you but I'm starving. Why don't you introduce me to the local pub? I heard they have an amazing inglenook fireplace there and serve a mean lunch."

"They do."

We share a smile and my heart flutters when it has no business doing so. I must remind myself this is strictly business and Luke is just being kind but as I follow him out of the room. I can't stop smiling.

CHAPTER 22
LUKE

This is an impossible situation, and every word Jessy spoke caused my heart to sink.

This will never work.

I'm not a businessman and never wanted to be. But Jessy is so enthusiastic and I'm guessing it has a lot to do with her deep love of the place. Her entire world is here and she can't bear the thought of change outside of the villager's control.

I already know the best thing for the village would be a huge multi-national snapping it up and having the cash to make it thrive again. However, that would spell the end of life as they know it because cheap rents and business opportunities in exchange for a few pots of jam won't cut it in the corporate world.

Jessy offered to drive us all to the pub but Morgana and Jasper were too busy plotting their show and Steven decided to keep an eye on them, so it left the two of us to speed off over the border into unchartered territory.

As we pass the rest of my estate, I fall in love a little

more as the pretty chocolate box cottages remind me of my responsibilities.

Jessy points out various sights and I'm particularly interested in a huge disused barn not far off the road.

"I wonder what that used to be?"

I voice my thoughts, staring at the rather grand structure that has grass and ivy apparently holding it up. It's set within a crumbling courtyard and Jessy says casually, "This was the stables for the house. It's one of the properties that could be converted to a residential dwelling."

"It could be magnificent."

"I agree."

The heater is struggling to warm our bones and I picture my own jeep back in Manchester that has heated seats and a state-of-the-art sound system. Jessy's car is extremely basic and rather small as it happens.

"You need a bigger car." I grumble as my boot takes up most of the room in the footwell and she giggles, a sound that brings a smile to my face, although I still don't know why.

"It suits me, but I don't transport six foot tall athletes with injuries very often, so you must excuse the confined space on offer."

"So, you don't have a boyfriend, then?"

I'm aware it's an inappropriate question given that I'm technically her boss, but I want to discover everything about her.

"Not really."

"What does that mean?"

"It means, I talk to a few guys on line and occasionally have a drink with one of them but nothing else."

"Several guys?"

I raise my eyes and she giggles. "A few."

I'm not sure why I hate the thought of that so much.

She changes the subject which doesn't escape me. "Tell me about Morgana. How did you meet?"

"Through Steven. "

"Your agent?"

"Yes. They were friends, and we were at the same party one night and the rest is history."

"How long have you been dating?"

I shift on the seat and say airily, "I don't remember exactly."

"Wow!" she laughs softly. "Don't let Morgana hear you say that. I bet if I asked her the same question, she would tell me the exact date and probably the time too."

I laugh. "You're probably right, nothing escapes her, and she's more clued up than people give her credit for."

"She is smart. I sense that already."

∿

Jessy pulls into the car park of a quaint village pub and says wistfully, "I've been coming here since I was a child."

"Wow, you start young in the country."

She rolls her eyes. "With my parents and my sister. Coke and crisps were all we were allowed, mainly in the beer garden, while we played on the swing."

She peers through the steamed-up window and rubs a gloved hand over it from the inside.

As we stare out at the welcoming pub, she sighs. "I missed it when I was at uni. I know everyone in it and it's a safe place to come on your own because inevitably there is someone you can sit with. There aren't many strangers in Granthaven and our neighbour Dream Valley."

"That sounds too good to be true."

"It is. The entire area is too good to be true because the people here rarely move on. Both communities work together and we use their high street in the absence of having one of our own."

She glances my way and cocks her head to one side. "They have a great Italian restaurant there. You should take Morgana. She would love it."

She smiles and as the light from the pub window catches her eye, it strikes me how pretty she looks. In fact, Jessy is one of the most beautiful women I have ever met, if not the most, and something shifts in the air between us and I can't tear my eyes away from her. It's a little awkward as I struggle to avert my gaze, so she does it for me as she says brightly, "Anyway, lunch. Come on, they serve great pub grub and if you like pints of beer, they have a local brew that is to die for."

"You drink beer?"

It amuses me and she nods. "Of course. Even the babies get a taste of it on their dummies. We are raised on the stuff."

I chuckle and as we head into the pub, I am very much looking forward to lunch.

∽

I RARELY GO TO PUBS, wine bars, or restaurants even. In Manchester, too many people recognise me and yet here it appears the only person they are interested in is Jessy.

We take ages to find a table, because she stops to

talk to nearly everyone and as she introduces me, I sense their curiosity. I love how nobody tells me how badly I played at the weekend, or that I missed an open goal. They don't want to talk about Morgana and take a selfie with me because they only know me as the guy who got lucky and inherited a village. I can tell by the look on their faces that is the only thing that impresses them.

"Hey! Up the Arsenal." A loud voice booms out and I jump as I spy Wilf Evans supping a pint at the bar, his trusty rifle propped up against his chair.

"Hey, Wilf." Jessy calls and I smile at him nervously.

"Hey, it's good to see you again."

I'm not sure it is, but he smiles a crooked smile, revealing he doesn't have many teeth left.

He calls out to anybody remotely interested.

"This is the guy I was telling you about. He's a personal friend of Wenger. Lucky sod."

A few murmurs accompany his statement and I want the ground to open up and swallow me as they disguise their smiles, knowing only too well I don't play for Arsenal.

Jessy giggles and says gently, "Good to see you, Wilf. We'll catch you later as this is a working lunch."

He taps his nose and winks. "If you say so, Jessy, darlin, your secret is safe with me."

Jessy's face flames as I chuckle softly.

As we take a table near the window, she gasps, "I'm so sorry. I'm sure nobody else is thinking that."

"It doesn't matter." I shrug. "I doubt there are paparazzi anywhere remotely near here and I haven't seen any phones pointed in our direction yet."

I lean forward and whisper, "If this was a secret affair, I doubt we would be here, anyway."

Jessy doesn't know where to look and grabs one of the menus from the table and says quickly, "They do a great burger, or a ploughman's, if you prefer something lighter."

"What are you having?"

"A burger. I need something hot inside me."

I raise my eyes and she giggles. "You've got a dirty mind, Mr Adams."

"I never said a thing, Miss Potter."

As we make our choices. Jessy heads to the bar and places our order and I insist on her paying with my credit card, reminding her it's a working lunch after all and we can put it down to expenses.

As she laughs at something the barmaid says, something shifts deep inside me. I love how natural she is. How comfortable I feel around her and it strikes me that Granthaven is weaving its magic spell around my heart as I realise I already hate the thought of leaving when the time comes.

CHAPTER 23
JESSY

I could have stayed at the Pigeon Trail all day because Luke is so easy to talk to. We chatted about life, our childhoods and what we love. It struck me how many things we have in common. Our love of thrillers on the television, dining out and rock music. He told me of many concerts he's been to of bands I would love to see live and movie premieres of films I can only catch up with when they reach the television. I loved hearing his tales of the club and the various places he has travelled to and how he made it so far.

One thing he doesn't talk about is his girlfriend and neither do I because I prefer not to think of him having one. Especially one as sweet and beautiful as Morgana, because it only reinforces the fact it will never be me.

∼

WE HEAD BACK to Granthaven and as soon as we step inside the door, the woman herself rushes to meet us.

"There you are."

She smiles at us both. "Did you have a good lunch? Was the food good?"

"It was great."

Luke slings his arm around her shoulder and gazes at her fondly and it causes a sudden drop to my heart. They look so happy as they gaze into one another's eyes and I get the impression I'm very much in the way.

Then Morgana flicks her gaze at me and says apologetically, "I'm so sorry, hun, Jasper wants us to do another interview for the camera. You can sit in if you like."

Luke nods. "You may enjoy it, Jessy. If we get this over with, we can make a start on the rooms afterwards."

"The rooms?" I'm confused, and he rolls his eyes.

"The inventory. We need to fleece this mansion to pay to stay. I could use your help."

Morgana shakes her head sadly. "I'm sorry you have to do that, hun. But needs must, I suppose."

She takes his arm and offers me a sad smile. "Luke and I will do everything in our power to save this village. We have a year to try at least, so if we all work together, we can achieve great things."

She whispers, "Leave it with me. I'll give it my best shot."

I watch as she pulls Luke away to the sitting room and as I follow them, I feel hollow inside. They make such a great couple and I can see why they fell in love. They are beautiful people inside and out, which somehow makes it worse. If she was entitled or full of her own self importance, I could happily hate her. The fact I like her boyfriend makes me the worst kind of human. I always considered myself a girl's girl but I'm sure if Luke gave me the green light, I would cut her up at the lights to reach him first.

Then there's the man himself.

What must it be like to be the main focus in his world? He makes me feel special just from a gentle look and soft smile in my direction. He acts interested in my life and listens when I speak. That is a powerful skill he possesses among several other ones and as I accept my place in their life, it doesn't stop me wishing things could be different.

∼

"What are your plans for Christmas?"

Jasper is reading questions from his phone as a camera man films the exquisite couple who look every inch the successful celebrities they are. Since we've been gone, the house has been filled with camera men, set designers, runners and production crew. It's another world, a fascinating one and I note there's even a make-up artist waiting nearby to add a touch of powder to their skin if the lights shine on them in the wrong way.

Morgana answers the question while smiling into the camera.

"Well, obviously, we spend it together. Usually at Luke's house in Cheshire, but this will be special because it's the first one in our new village."

Luke nods, gazing at Morgana with a soft expression.

"I never appreciated how special Christmas could be because I'm always working, but obviously this year is different for many different reasons."

He points to his boot and Morgana says sweetly, "It

was a blessing in disguise for me because now I get him all to myself."

"Will you be entertaining this Christmas?" Jasper asks and Morgana nods enthusiastically.

"Of course. Since coming to Granthaven we have been made aware of a legend that I am keen to resurrect."

I lean forward as she says with a wistful expression. "Many years ago, the Lord and Lady threw a Christmas Eve party for all the villagers. It was back in the days before televisions and the modern age and women were expected to marry rather than have careers."

She raises her eyes and grins. "Well, obviously things are different now but back then the house was decorated with mistletoe and if a young girl from the village was caught and kissed under the mistletoe, if she refused, she wouldn't receive any marriage proposals for a year."

She rolls her eyes. "Like that would work today, but back then it was the most important thing to a young woman of age. Then one night the lady of the manor died on Christmas Eve and all the mistletoe in Granthaven died with her and has never grown again."

She pauses for theatrical effect and whispers, "The legend says that only when the lady of the house receives true love's kiss will happiness return to Granthaven and the mistletoe will grow once again."

She turns to Luke and kisses him softly on the cheek and says lightly, "I'm hoping to steal a kiss myself this Christmas Eve and I'm having some mistletoe shipped in for luck. My greatest wish is to bring the heart back to Granthaven and revive the fortunes of a village that has suffered from neglect over the years."

I'm not sure if I agree with her description, but I can't

fault her intentions and my heart sinks when I picture Luke and Morgana kissing under the imported mistletoe on Christmas Eve with the world watching.

Will he propose? Will there be a wedding at the small church nearby that we will all be invited to attend? If so just kill me now because I already know if that happened, it would certainly be a miserable day for me.

∽

THE QUESTIONS LASTED for another hour, along with several takes of filming to get the perfect shot and as the crew wrap up the shoot, Luke heads my way with a grimace.

"I hate this circus, but it's Morgana's world. Hopefully, we will drum up some sponsorship with her shameless plugs peppered through the dialogue."

"I must hand it to her. She knew what she was doing." I admit as we walk into the hallway and Luke nods. "She is the most savvy woman I know. It's why she's so successful. Knowing her, she will have several offers of sponsorship by the end of the day and even more by Christmas Eve itself. Check the internet tomorrow because it will be full of stories of this place and her story."

"Then you should strike while the iron's hot."

"I don't understand." He cocks his head to one side.

"Set up a crowd funding campaign, so if anyone wants to donate to saving Granthaven, they can."

His eyes light up and I say with animation. "You could set it up for the restoration of the church, the village hall and some of the more dilapidated cottages. Perhaps to develop the farm shop, or one of the other things we have spoken about. Think about it, Luke." I face him with more animation than I've had since I was a young girl waiting for Santa on Christmas Eve.

"This may work. It's worth a try, at least."

"I think you've hit on something, Jessy."

To my surprise, he reaches out and lifts me up, spinning me around while I laugh out loud.

As we stop and he places my feet on the ground, I'm conscious that his arms are still firmly clasped around my waist. For a moment, we stare into one another's eye and I detect a yearning in his that must be a reflection of my own. The silence is awkward between us as we say nothing at all and it's as if time stands still.

A sudden movement makes us pull apart and I lower my eyes to disguise the guilt in them as Steven grumbles, "Bloody club. They want to send their doctor to check on your foot. He arrives tomorrow and needs a bed while he organises your physio regime."

"But that's good, though." Luke says and I detect the hope in his voice as Steven sighs. "I suppose so, but it doesn't leave you much time to rest. Once those guys get hold of you, you won't have time for anything else."

"It will be fine."

Luke sounds sure of that, but it reminds me of who he is and his real job and my heart sinks. Luke is here on borrowed time and if I'm to protect my heart, I must admit to myself that whatever is happening between us is business and nothing more.

CHAPTER 24
LUKE

Jessy is quiet, unusually so and I hope it wasn't because of my inappropriate behaviour in the hall before Steven interrupted a moment that shocked me as much as it apparently did her. I'm not sure what Steven will think of it. Not that he would tell me, anyway. He keeps his thoughts to himself most of the time, but he misses nothing. He will wonder why I'm so drawn to a complete stranger who I've only just met, and I couldn't even tell him if he asked. I have no idea – but I like Jessy Potter and I don't know why.

We head into the study of what I'm assuming was the late Lord Townsend because its masculine interior would never be the choice for a woman.

Jessy stares around with interest as I turn on the small light suspended over a wooden desk that has several water marks and scratches deeply ingrained within the wood.

"Why are we here?" She asks, more with interest than

suspicion, and I point to the huge oil painting in a gold frame above the stone fireplace.

"I wanted to check this landscape out. It could be worth something."

"Luke."

Jessy rolls her eyes and laughs softly. "If you consider we are the best people to trip around your home and value it, you're very much mistaken."

"What do you suggest?"

"Calling in a professional, of course."

"Who would probably rip me off."

"Why would they do that?"

"Because people do when you have money. They value services higher and things for sale lower."

"Not in my world, they don't." Jessy's expression softens, and she appears worried.

"I never thought of it like that. It can't be nice thinking the worst of people."

"You get used to it. If anything, it's best because then you're not disappointed when they prove you were right all along."

We stand side by side and stare at the magnificent landscape and Jessy adds, "I wonder who painted this?"

She peers closer and then laughs softly.

"What?"

I move beside her and stare at the scrawling signature at the bottom of the painting and chuckle, "Well, this painting is going nowhere, then."

"It appears the lady of the house was a keen artist. She was good, though."

Jessy reaches out and runs her finger over the signature and appears thoughtful.

"A lot of artists live in Dorset. The surroundings are an endless source of inspiration."

"It is very beautiful."

I can't stop staring at her as she loses herself in her thoughts, giving me time to outline every one of her features in my mind for later. Since meeting her, Jessy hasn't left my thoughts for long. I am fascinated by her quiet beauty, her soft smiles and honest expression. What you see, you get with Jessy Potter and I am definitely not used to that.

"I'm curious, Luke." She whispers, as she gazes at the painting, apparently somewhere else in her mind.

"About what?"

"Why you inherited the estate? I mean, I hope that isn't rude, but I don't believe you're related to the Townsend's at all by blood and I was under the illusion that only blood relatives could inherit Granthaven."

I lean back against the desk and sigh.

"My father is – sorry, was – Lady Townsend's brother. They fell out several years ago for reasons I was never told. Anyway, Lady Townsend, Christabel, my aunt, married the Lord, but they never had children of their own. His own brother died of cancer before he could provide an heir, so the line stopped with my aunt's husband. She was never going to leave this place to my father and I suppose, out of spite, left it to me instead, although I'm guessing it would have been more vengeful if she had left him to deal with this."

I shake my head against the pity in Jessy's eyes. "Don't feel bad for me. I know it sucks being left thirty million pounds' worth of misery. Life's a bitch along with the tax man."

"The tax man?"

I blow out a huff of frustration. "If I'm right, the tax owed on my inheritance is several million pounds before I can even begin to bring the properties back to life. Add it to the costs of the restorations makes for many sleepless nights."

"I was wondering about that."

Jessy moves and leans against the desk and we stare at the painting as we contemplate the madness of my life right now.

"You should speak to your estate manager, Geoffrey Knight. He will have access to the information you need."

"What information?"

Jessy turns to me and I experience an incredible urge to reach out and tuck a stray piece of her hair away from her face and as I wonder how she will react to that, she says carefully, "Inheritance tax only applies to the profits or the amount left after all the debts are taken into consideration. Granthaven may not have many debts, or it may have many. Geoffrey would know and be able to give you a ball park figure about the state of the accounts."

"Why are you so clever, Jessy?"

She raises her eyes. "I'm not clever, Luke. It's just an area I studied in for the past four years. It's fresh in my mind, but I don't understand how things work – not really."

"You know more than me though, which proves that I did the right thing in appointing you as my business manager."

"You may regret that decision."

The soft curve of her lips is all I can think of, and her

business brain is definitely not the first thing I'm picturing right now. I'm overwhelmed by the urge to kiss her, but she sighs, turns away, and after gazing at the painting and taking a deep breath, she says resolutely, "Okay." You call Geoffrey and set up a meeting, and I'll spend the afternoon drawing up a business plan."

"Why?"

I must have missed something here, and she says firmly, "Because you must make a business plan, Luke. It may be necessary to approach the bank for a loan, mortgage or anything along those lines. Investment is what you need and we can't rely on crowdfunding to restore the village. If you are serious about this, you must act on it and while I'm at it, I'll look into the logistics of setting the campaign up online. There is a lot to do."

She moves away from the desk and smiles apologetically. "I'm sorry, it's a lot to think about and I expect you've got more important things on your mind, like your ankle. Leave this with me and I'll report back when I've done my homework."

She peers around and then says softly, "If something is worth the struggle, nothing else matters and you do everything in your power to make it successful."

She swings her eyes back to me and I note the hardened edge in hers as she says with determination.

"Leave it with me. I'll work out a plan and if we fail, it won't be because we didn't try."

She smiles. "If that's everything, I'll leave you in peace."

She is waiting for an answer and I want mine to be, 'No! That is definitely not everything because I don't want you to leave.' If she does, she will be on my mind anyway and I hate the desperation in my voice as I say quickly, "But you'll be back later on today."

"Why?" She is genuinely confused and I search for any sane reason why she must be. "Because of the meeting with Geoffrey. I need you here to take, um, notes."

"But you haven't even arranged it, and Geoffrey may be busy."

Her eyes widen with confusion and I flash her a blinding smile. "Shall we say four pm back here in this study?"

"Okay, not a problem, but text me if he can't make it."

She spins on her heels and as she leaves the room, my heart trails after her like a lovesick puppy.

CHAPTER 25
JESSY

Well, that was odd, but I don't have time to think about it when I note Angie heading my way with a troubled expression on her face.

"Jessy." She whispers as she hurries towards me and grabs my arm.

"Let's get out of here. We really need to talk."

She rushes with speed towards the front door and as we spill through it and it closes behind us with a resounding thud, she drags me in the direction of the lake and says with a low whistle, "You will never guess what I just saw."

"What?"

Angie has always been overly dramatic so it may be anything and she whispers, "Morgana booked me to do her nails and I arrived about ten minutes early because I was excited and couldn't wait to get there. So–" Her words are tripping over themselves and I stop and say pointedly, "Calm down, what did you see?"

"I'm telling you." She rolls her eyes – as I said, so dramatic.

"Well, Karen let me in and told me I'd find Morgana in the main bedroom because it had the light, apparently." She rolls her eyes. "Anyway, I went that way and I was a bit nervous. I'm not going to lie because that house is kind of creepy if you ask me and the paintings appeared to be watching me."

She stops. "Do you think it's haunted because I wouldn't be shocked if it was? I mean, so much tragedy must have left a few stray souls wandering the halls for closure."

I laugh. "Focus, Angie. I doubt the place is haunted. So, what did you discover – a ghost perhaps?"

"If only."

She groans and glances around her before lowering her voice.

"Worse than a ghost. I witnessed a sin."

"A sin?"

I'm wondering if Angie has lost her mind because who sees sin? Is there such a thing, anyway?

"I didn't knock and opened the bedroom door, expecting Morgana to be sitting at the dressing table, revelling in the appropriate light for the occasion, but it wasn't the light she was revelling in."

"Explain."

Now I'm interested because the words 'revelling' and 'bedroom' are conjuring up all kinds of images and Angie whispers, "I found her hugging that agent guy, Steven and I heard her say she wished things were different and they could be together."

"Angie!"

I gasp in shock and she nods, her eyes laden with worry as she whispers, "He was reassuring her. Telling her it had to be this way and things will change when the time is right."

She pauses for dramatic effect and gasps, "Then he kissed her – on the lips no less and not the kind of kiss you give to a friend or family member, if you know what I'm saying."

"Did they see you?"

Angie shakes her head. "No. I backed out of there pretty damn quickly and then knocked loudly on the door and when she called me in that Steven guy had gone."

"Where did he go?"

"Who knows? Possibly through a secret passage or a connecting room door. How do I know and Morgana just squealed in her excitable way and told me she was happy to see me because one of her nails had chipped and she couldn't stop looking at it. That it was spoiling her day and she couldn't see past it"

"Her chipped nail?" I pull a face. "I would have thought that was the least of her problems."

Angie nods. "She carried on as if nothing had happened and told me how happy they were to be here and she even filmed us for her vlog."

"I bet you loved that."

I know my friend so well and Angie shrugs, looking pleased with herself.

"I mean, obviously when the video goes up I will repost it with some kind of friends emoji and tag her, so her followers see I'm her new bestie."

She shakes her head. "Anyway, that's beside the point.

Do you think Luke knows she is lusting after another man and has she lost her freaking mind because that Steven guy is nowhere near as dishy as Luke Adams, premier league hottie?"

I must agree with her, but then I remember the wistful glances we have shared and the way he stares into my eyes as if he wants to say something but can't. The impromptu hug and the sexual tension between us and I say fearfully, "Oh no."

"What?"

Angie spins me around and I gasp, "What if they're, well, in an open relationship? Swingers even!"

"No way!"

Angie's eyes widen even further and even the ducks on the lake start screaming, or the equivalent in duck language, as we face the possibility that our new landlords may be about to turn Granthaven into Sodom and Gomorrah.

"What happened?"

Angie isn't my friend by chance. She actually can read my mind and I say with horror interwoven through my sentences, "What if he wants me to, well, do other less regular duties?"

Angie shakes her head slowly. "Wow, you lucky bitch."

We both burst out laughing because she's not wrong and I shrug. "So what if they're prone to decorating their doors with upside down pineapples."

Angie nods. "It would certainly alleviate the boredom around here."

"Imagine the memories."

"Yes, and the headlines if it ever got out. We would be famous."

"Infamously famous." I remind her, and she grins.

"It would be worth it, though. Imagine the fun we would have."

We giggle like two teenagers as our conversation tumbles down the nearest rabbit hole and for the entire journey home, it is all we can talk about.

CHAPTER 26
LUKE

It didn't take much to persuade Geoffrey Knight to hop in his car and meet me at four o'clock and as we wait for Jessy, I take stock of a man who is a definite stereotype.

Geoffrey is in his late fifties, rather overweight, his large extended stomach restrained inside a buttoned up waistcoat of the checked variety. Paired with a well-tailored tweed jacket, crisp shirt, and polished leather brogues, reflecting an understated elegance.

His sandy coloured hair is peppered with grey, which adds to his distinguished appearance and I'm guessing he enjoys activities such as hunting, fishing and shooting.

He is a definitive stereotype with his ruddy complexion and twinkling eyes, his loud voice booming and his aftershave resembling the scent of brandy.

"Mr Adams, I was so sad to hear of Lady Townsend's passing. We spent many happy hours in this same room disposing of a bottle of vintage brandy while we put the world to rights."

I don't doubt that for a second and say guiltily, "Thank you. I may not be able to put the world to rights, but I could offer you a glass of brandy."

I notice the bottle on the dusty bookcase and some glasses nestling behind the glass cupboard and he smiles pompously. "Well, it's a little early, but I don't mind if I do."

As I hobble over to the cabinet he says loudly, "Tough luck on your injury. I hope it heals soon."

"It's fine, just a little cumbersome."

I pour the brandy into the glasses and consider adding a third before the door opens and Jessy hurries inside.

"I'm so sorry I'm late."

Geoffrey says in surprise, "I don't understand."

Jessy holds out her hand to his. "Jessy Potter, Mr Knight. I'm Luke's business advisor, trainee actually, and he asked if I minded taking notes because it will probably be a lot for him to take in."

I catch her eye and smile, biting back the chuckle that her words have caused. She's not wrong, although the real reason I wanted her here may shock her more, so I splash some brandy into the third glass and hand them to my guests.

"Really?" She raises her eyes and my fingers brush against hers as she accepts the glass and I nod toward Geoffrey, causing understanding to dawn in her eyes.

As we take our seats, Geoffrey withdraws a notebook from his briefcase and lays it out on the desk before taking a sip of brandy and unbuttoning his waistcoat.

His self-contained paunch visibly relaxes over his belt and he sighs with relief.

"Now we're comfortable, we can begin."

He fixes me with an autocratic frown.

"Granthaven has very few secrets and many problems."

My heart sinks and Jessy speaks up. "I'm sorry to interrupt, Mr Knight, but Mr Adams is facing a huge inheritance tax bill for the estate and the most important thing on the agenda is how he can raise the money to pay the tax man."

Geoffrey raises his eyes and stares at me with a thoughtful expression.

"I see."

He flips open his leather-bound notebook and appears to be searching for something, and Jessy shrugs as she smiles at me apologetically.

"Here it is." He says triumphantly and scans the page before stabbing a thick finger against a set of figures.

"Lady Townsend raised the same subject herself at one of our delightful meetings. It was soon after her husband, the late Lord Townsend, died and she had similar concerns."

I lean forward. "What happened?"

Geoffrey takes another gulp of brandy and glances at the bottle with a brisk, "I'm a little dry, Mr Adams. Perhaps a little more to wet my whistle would be agreeable."

Jessy springs forward and splashes more brandy into Geoffrey's glass and he smiles his appreciation.

"Super."

Once again, he knocks back the alcohol and says with satisfaction, "Ah, yes, the tax. Luckily for her, the lord had anticipated that eventuality and made provision in his will for the sum to be paid out of his fortune to the Inland Revenue, meaning his wife could mourn him in private without the distasteful subject of money as a distraction."

"So, he had the money saved."

Luke sounds impressed and Geoffrey nods, knocking back the rest of the glass and staring pointedly at the bottle.

Jessy wastes no time in refilling his glass for the third time and this time she is more generous and his eyes gleam as he takes the glass from her hand and says gruffly, "Apparently, it was tradition and enabled Granthaven to remain in the family without the need for the unpleasant scenario of selling any of the properties, or land to appease the government."

Jessy's eyes meet mine and I sense the confusion in hers and say evenly, "So, I could sell some of my collateral to pay what I owe?"

I never believed that was an option because when the solicitor read the will, my inheritance was under strict conditions. I was forbidden to sell any of the assets and must live in the house for one year before it would be possible to list the entire estate as a whole or not at all.

"Good God no," Geoffrey says, slightly shocked and Jessy huffs with frustration as she takes her seat again.

"There will be no dividing up the estate under the conditions of the trust."

"The trust?" I'm getting a headache and Geoffrey nods, obviously relishing being the only person here who knows what the hell is going on.

"No, Granthaven comes as a package and always will

as laid down by the terms of the trust one of the more far-sighted lords set up."

"So, the tax?" Jessy reminds him, appearing to be losing the will to live, and Geoffrey nods.

"Is already paid."

I stare at him in shock and Jessy says in disbelief. "How?"

Geoffrey consults his notebook. "Lady Townsend was saving the rent from the houses, the farm and the various other business interests and placed it in a holding company entitled Townsend enterprises."

I stare at Jessy in confusion, and Geoffrey nods toward the brandy bottle. "I don't suppose–"

Once again, Jessy sprints to the cabinet and grabs the bottle, placing it down on the desk and saying quickly, "Please, help yourself."

The gleam in Geoffrey's eyes is slightly worrying and I wonder if I'm feeding his alcohol addiction as he tosses a generous amount of the bottle into his ever-draining glass.

"Yes, she was extremely frugal and managed to amass the exact amount I believe was owed to HMRC."

The relief I feel is enormous and I sag against the back of my seat as Geoffrey booms, "She believed in her husband's business acumen and took steps to reciprocate it. You have no outstanding debts and can rest assured your inheritance is secure."

I speak up. "I'm sorry, Geoffrey, but I'm a little confused."

He takes another sip of brandy and fixes his sharp eyes on me as I add, "My aunt was sitting on millions of pounds, but the estate was left to decay. She could have used the income to restore the village."

"Why would she do that?" Geoffrey shakes his head. "Then your inheritance would be worth more and you'd be forced to sell half of it to pay the dues owed."

He leans forward and fixes me with a steadfast look.

"You can't have it all, Mr Adams. You can have the whole shebang and all the problems that brings, or let it dwindle to nothing over the years as its prosperity places value on the inheritance, subsequently bleeding into the government's back account and not into yours."

He leans back and shrugs. "Progress is not always the best thing. History, tradition and the simple pleasures are worth way more than that. Think about it, Mr Adams, before you embark on a mission to save this magical place. Perhaps it doesn't need saving after all and, in fact, is well placed to be the one to save you instead."

Silence accompanies his words, and he turns the page on his notebook and says with a low chuckle, "So, let me bring you up to speed with the present state of the economy in Granthaven, but first, can I offer anyone else a splash of brandy and if so, we could really use another bottle."

CHAPTER 27
JESSY

To use an old-fashioned word that my grandmother used a lot – I am flabbergasted. After Geoffrey dropped his bombshell, I could scarcely concentrate on the rest of the meeting and I doubt Luke could either. Geoffrey droned on about rental agreements, bills that were growing by the day and obligations to the community that made my head spin.

If Luke was having doubts before, he must have made his mind up now because this is an impossible situation. Granthaven will only remain the place I love if it's left to exist rather than prosper. It's a lot to think about, not only for Luke but also for the rest of us because if we push for change, we may not like what that involves.

Geoffrey staggers to the door when the meeting ends in a haze of brandy fumes and as he leaves, I say with a frown, "Please don't tell me he drove here?"

Luke heads to the window that overlooks the driveway and groans.

"There's an old Jag parked outside that definitely doesn't belong here. Should someone take his keys?"

"If Wilf was here, we could get him to shoot out his tyres." I add with a grin, and Luke gasps, "You said his gun wasn't loaded."

"I lied."

The expression on Luke's face causes me to laugh out loud and as we watch Geoffrey heave his body into the driver's seat of the Jag, I have a real fear that we should call the police.

"Where does he live?" Luke asks and I reply, "Dream Valley."

Luke grabs his phone and, after a short while, says casually, "Steven, the guy who just left, needs a lift. He's had too much to drink. Can somebody drive him home and grab a taxi back?"

He cuts the call and we watch as Steven races out of the house and waves Geoffrey down as the car begins to move away and after a brief conversation, they swap places and head off out of the property.

"Does everyone do what you ask them to?" I ask, and Luke shrugs. "Not everyone." He chuckles. "Morgana does what she likes and never asks my opinion. If I had one, she would pretend to consider it and then disregard it, anyway."

My heart drops at the mention of his girlfriend and I wonder if I should say something. Then again, it's none of my business and so I say brightly, "Anyway, it appears you have a huge decision to make."

"Apparently so."

He gazes out of the window with a thoughtful expression and then says, "What do you think?"

"I don't know. To be honest, it's an impossible situation, although something did strike me when he was speaking."

"What?"

Luke turns to me and his eyes light with interest as I say carefully, "It makes sense now."

"What does?"

"Business."

He arches his brow and I take my seat and prop my elbows on the desk and stare at him.

"Granthaven has no debts – allegedly. They take the money in but rarely spend any, unless it's on bills or urgent repairs."

"I suppose."

He takes his seat opposite me and stares directly into my eyes as I speak. "It's a strange way to run a business because this is exactly that – a business. Most ones I know operate on borrowed money. Credit if you like. The income pays for the outgoings and there isn't much left to sit in their banks at the end of the month."

"Surely that's bad, though."

"Not really, if you consider it another way. They use the money generated to plough back into the business. They grow rather than shrink and at the end of the year their debts offset their profits, generating a low tax bill."

Luke's eyes gleam. "I see what you mean, but surely it just increases the value of the business when it's time to pay inheritance tax."

"Not if the individual doesn't inherit the entire business on a personal level."

"I don't understand."

Luke appears confused and I say carefully, "I'm not

saying this is correct, but what if you made Granthaven a business? A limited company with shareholders but maintain the controlling interest. That way, the business remains in your family, but the profits are shared. When you pass on, it's only your share of that business that will be liable, but if the debts outweigh the profits, there would be less to pay."

"I see."

Luke is thoughtful and I say quickly, "I may be wrong and there must be reasons against that, but it's worth appointing an expert to look into it for you."

Luke nods and then sighs as he leans back, the empty bottle of brandy reminding us that sometimes we all need a little shot of Dutch courage. Some more than others.

I glance at my watch.

"I should be going. The rehearsals are tonight and I need to eat first and mum is waiting with her shepherd's pie."

"Is the rehearsal still happening here?"

Luke asks with a sympathetic smile and I nod miserably.

"I believe it is. That was so generous of, um, Morgana, to offer your home to us. It certainly makes a difference because the village hall resembles a deep freeze right now."

Luke nods and glances out of the window at the darkening shadows outside.

"Will you be okay walking home? It's dark outside."

"Of course." I roll my eyes. "This is the safest place on earth."

I falter and say sadly, "For now, anyway."

As I stand, I smile at Luke warmly. "I don't envy your predicament. Money doesn't always bring happiness and you are facing some big decisions. If I can help in any way, please ask. I'll try my best, but I really believe you need a professional now."

As I make to leave, Luke says with laughter in his voice, "I'll see you later, Jessy."

"You're coming to the rehearsal?"

My heart sinks as he winks. "I wouldn't miss it for the world."

CHAPTER 28
LUKE

Geoffrey Knight gave me a lot to consider. It seems like a mammoth task – an impossible one because I don't have time for this. If I'm honest, I just want to get better and return to the club where all my thinking is done for me.

I live a charmed life in Cheshire. I'm paid well – too much really and my life is spent between the training ground and the stadiums where I do my best to make my team proud.

I'm not a landowner. I don't run country estates and am responsible for actual human beings. It scares the hell out of me – of making a decision that affects so many lives and I hate myself for even considering abandoning them in their hour of need.

Then there's Jessy. She lives here – not in Cheshire; not even close. But how can I keep her in my life? I'm with Morgana. We are a partnership.

Steven soon returns from Dream Valley and heads my way with an irritated scowl. "It's a good job you warned me about that guy. He stank of booze and if he had come across anything in the road, he could be up on a murder charge. Honestly, Luke, you should be more careful with your hospitality. The last thing we need is a court case naming you as responsible."

He sighs heavily. "Colin, the physio, is arriving tomorrow lunchtime. At least you won't have to wear your boot much longer."

"Thank God."

He peers at me with concern.

"Are you worried about your ankle?"

"A little. I haven't given it much thought."

"Because of this place?" He appears thoughtful, and I nod.

"It's a problem that keeps getting, well, even more problematic."

"Due to your responsibilities, or something else?"

He studies me carefully and I realise what he's trying to ask. It's Jessy. He senses my interest in her, and that doesn't surprise me. Steven doesn't say much, but he's observant and definitely not a fool and I confess. "I like her."

"I thought so." He jerks his head towards the kitchen.

"Come and tell me all about it, but I need a strong coffee first after that journey from hell."

As we walk through the dusty, decaying house, it only reinforces the huge mountain before me. It could be amazing given a few million thrown at it and it strikes me that a few million is what my house in Cheshire cost me. As I said, I get paid a lot and don't have much to spend my money on and as we head inside the kitchen, I see it for what it could be and not what it is now.

Steven wastes no time in flicking on the kettle and nods toward the wooden chair in the corner.

"So, Jessy."

He shakes his head and huffs out a breath, mirroring my own state of mind.

"We knew this was going to happen one day." He says, running his fingers through his hair, which tells me he's agitated and I nod, sharing his concern.

The kettle boils and as he makes the coffee, I stare out of the window at the view of the lake in the distance and picture this as a family home rather than one where ghosts patrol the building as a nod to happier times in the past.

Steven places the coffee before me and takes his seat, nursing the mug between his hands and shivering slightly. "Imagine the heating bill in this place when it does get one installed. It's a lot, Luke, and as your agent and your friend, I want you to consider your decision extremely carefully."

"You think this is the wrong one, don't you?" I ask, peering at him closely, noticing for the first time the weary lines around his eyes.

"Not necessarily."

He leans back and says thoughtfully, "You deserve to be happy, Luke, it's all any of us want for you but your life isn't here. It's half way up the country and you must devote all your time to that. The life of a footballer can be a short one and you must capitalise on it while you can. Make solid investments for your future and yet above all else, remain grounded and don't allow yourself to be caught up with the wrong people and then make the wrong decisions."

"Thanks, man."

I'm a little emotional because Steven, despite his role in my life, has always had my best interests at heart.

He raises his eyes, "But Jessy. That's a problem I never saw coming."

"And I did?"

He smiles briefly. "Does she like you?"

"I'm not sure. It's hardly something I can ask her. Why would she think of me in that way, especially with Morgana living under the same roof?"

He chuckles softly. "She's always been a problem."

As if she heard us, the woman herself heads our way with Jasper in tow and says loudly, "Well, we're finally getting somewhere."

They pull up seats at the table and she beams at us.

"The production team has worked a small miracle already and Jasper and I have had a successful day filming some segments for the show. Tonight, the pantomime rehearsals will provide more footage and our plan to showcase the village will be on schedule."

She turns to me and smiles sweetly, "So, with your permission, I would like to arrange the Christmas Eve party. It will take a lot of organising, so I must get on it right away."

She turns to Jasper, already anticipating my agreement. "We will make lists, lots of glorious lists and research local caterers and event planners. I'm picturing a twelve foot tree in the entrance hall with lots of fairy lights everywhere. They are so magical, aren't they?"

She doesn't even stop for breath and continues with animation. "The theme must be festive red and green with some accents of white. We will raid the gardens and woods for foliage and I'll do a vlog on decorating at Christmas. I'll also prime my Instagram account and do several stories – possibly run a competition. We must have carols with lovely villagers in bobble hats and carrying lanterns. I can just picture the scene."

I sip my coffee and let her words wash over me as I picture how cute Jessy looks in her red bobble hat. I can see her now singing like an angel as I stare at her in adoration.

"Luke!"

Morgana's sharp use of my name brings me back to the conversation.

"What?"

"Do you agree?"

"To the party, of course."

She rolls her eyes. "No, darling, you haven't been listening, have you?"

"To what?" I notice Steven's expression and wonder what I've missed because it appears the jokes on me as Jasper bites back a grin.

"The pantomime silly."

Morgana rolls her eyes. "You must play the lord."

"But they have a lord and a lady. We can't take their roles. It would be wrong."

"I'm not saying that. Honestly, Luke, keep up will you. No–" She pauses for breath and then smiles broadly. "Jasper says it will be so cool if I took over the production and they filmed me organising the entire thing. You will play the lord opposite Jessy's lady and the previous lord can be let off the hook."

"What hook?" I shrivel in my seat as Jasper adds,

"He's nervous about appearing on film as he plays a part he never wanted in the first place."

"How do you know all of this?"

I'm stunned and Jasper adds, "He pulled me aside and had a word. He's a good lad but would rather be down the pub rather than playing opposite someone he considers as a sister. He doesn't want to be a laughingstock, his words not mine, and would prefer not to feature in any filming."

"And you think I would?"

Morgana rolls her eyes. "You're already participating in the filming, Luke and I don't know what the problem is. You are kind of the lord for real, anyway. Not by title, but by default, and Jessy seems a nice girl, so how hard will it be?"

I catch Steven's eye and we are both painfully aware exactly how hard it will be because, with Morgana watching, along with the entire world, it will be extremely difficult to hide the feelings that are developing fast for my intoxicating business advisor.

CHAPTER 29
JESSY

I can't believe Scott has thrown me under the bus like this.

Angie tells me the news as we walk to rehearsals.

"So, where does that leave me?"

I stare at her in dismay and she shrugs. "Pray to God they don't cast Mr Spalding as the lord. There isn't much choice other than him."

"Then I'll pull out." I make a face. "There is no way I'm kissing him under the mistletoe. He could be my grandad."

"I'm sorry, Jessy. Mum tried to talk Scott back into it, but he was adamant and you know what he's like when he digs his heels in."

My heart sinks because Angie isn't wrong. Most of the time, Scott is easygoing and would do anything to keep the peace, but he's also very determined and won't do anything he is uncomfortable with.

"It was the thought of being filmed that freaked him

out." Angie moans. "You know how he hates being in front of the camera, even for photographs. I'm sorry, Jessy, this is a disaster."

"Well, if Mr Spalding so much as looks my way when they ask for volunteers, I'm calling it quits too. I didn't even want to do this stupid pantomime. It's the last thing I wanted."

We reach Granthaven Manor and Angie says reassuringly. "It won't be so bad. Something will come up, it always does."

We head through the front door and into the now warm and inviting hallway and Angie sighs. "This is so much better. I can't believe what they've already done to the place."

I nod my agreement because it appears that having a production company at your disposal can work miracles, and I note the warm lighting that has replaced the flickering bulbs. Polished surfaces gleam and the floor has been cleaned to reveal the intricacies of the parquet flooring. It even smells fantastic and I wonder if they are pumping pine scented fragrance into the air by machine because it is fresh and clean and nothing like the dusty, slightly musty smell of before.

Jasper waves at us from the sitting room doorway.

"Come in, come in. There is some mulled wine for everyone to chase away the chill of winter and the fire is heating the room nicely."

As we almost run to get to the mulled wine, Jasper hangs back and says quickly as I make to pass him, "May I have a quick word, Jessy?"

My heart sinks because he appears edgy, which can only mean one thing. I won't like what's coming and I steel myself to pull out quicker than Angie is heading for the wine if I don't like what he says.

The door closes behind her and effectively cuts off the gentle murmur of conversation in the room and Jasper smiles.

"Just a heads up that your leading man has changed. I wanted to tell you before you went inside to prepare you in advance. They are filming the rehearsal tonight and I don't want any expressions caught by the camera that I haven't prepared for."

He rolls his eyes. "We don't have the time or the energy to re-take a scene and I always feel as if the spontaneity goes out of the shot when the actors have gone over it several times already."

"We're not actors, Jasper."

I am slightly miffed that our pantomime is being commandeered to suit the newcomers, and Jasper smiles reassuringly. "Of course, my darling, but humour me please."

He takes a deep breath. "Anyway, your dashing lord will now be played by our very own lord and master, Luke Adams."

"Excuse me?"

I sense the blood draining from my face as I understand why Jasper has prepared me, because the horror on my face would not make for a pleasurable scene in the show.

"But–"

"I know, amazing, isn't it? He took some persuading but realised the show must go on and he must grin and bear it for the good of the reality show. Oh, and there is another small change that you should be aware of."

"What?"

My legs are weak at the mere thought of kissing Luke because that is the only thing I can focus on right now. This is a disaster. Kissing Scott was bad enough due to the fact I consider him family more than anything, but kissing Luke is a completely different thing entirely – because I want to. More than anything, but it will be televised. The entire world will have access to my infatuation and I will struggle to disguise that.

Then Jasper makes things one hundred times worse when he says triumphantly, "And the best new is that Morgana will be directing."

"Wait, what?"

I stare at him in shock as he claps his hands with excitement. "Yes, she will direct and it will make for such a good segment in our show. She is a natural for the camera and has great vision. You are lucky to have her because your production of whatever the thing is called will go down in history as the greatest show ever."

He nods towards the sitting room.

"Anyway, paint on your excited smile, darling. It's time to face the cameras and I guess every woman and some men out there will consider you the luckiest woman alive this Christmas, so I would be very appreciative if you could act like it."

He flings the door open, and it's as if a spotlight is thrown on me as I walk inside in a confused daze, the stares of the villagers and production crew firmly fixed on me as I walk into the room. There is even a camera recording it and I attempt to act normally, but inside I'm a nervous wreck.

I will be kissing Luke under the direction of his girlfriend and the entire world will have a front-row seat.

Angie heads straight to my side and thrusts a glass of mulled wine in my hand and whispers, "Well, talk about a Christmas miracle. Why didn't I say I'd be the lady this year? I got Edward Cummins as my lord and you get Luke freaking gorgeous Adams as yours. Why is life so unfair?"

I say nothing and knock back the wine for medicinal reasons, wishing that bottle of brandy was at hand instead because, as sure as I'm in my worst nightmare right now, I am finally realising the power of an alcoholic haze.

CHAPTER 30
LUKE

The expression on Jessy's face says it all.

She hates this.

Jasper went outside to forewarn her and as she walked into the room, I saw it in her eyes. She is upset. I can tell by the way her smile is frozen in place and the fear in her usually sparkling eyes.

Great. My infatuation is definitely one-sided and I'm the guy who must try to act normally as I step forward to kiss the one woman I can't stop thinking about. To make matters even worse, Morgana will be directing it and filming it for posterity. A harsh reminder that despite what everyone thinks, the famous Luke Adams really can't have everything he wants in life.

Jessy sits on the couch beside her friend and appears to be in shock. She won't even meet my eye and Steven whispers, "This should be interesting."

"You think."

Morgana claps her hands and I must admit makes a cute director with her script in hand and her hair tied up in a messy bun, her attitude glasses – she doesn't need them to see – perched on the end of her nose, her manicured fingernails clutching the pen that is poised and ready for action.

"Darlings. We will make this the most amazing pantomime ever. Now, let's start at the beginning and see what we can come up with."

I exhale sharply because, quite frankly, this is my worst nightmare. Firstly, I'm not comfortable with any of this. Learning lines is not my strongest point and acting, well, I'm a better footballer. Morgana has pre-empted my excuses and the production team were instructed to hold boards with my lines on them behind the camera, so I can read them rather than memorise them and as the main star of the show is the gorgeous Jessy, I can sit back and watch her with nobody thinking it's strange.

The villagers appear a little star-struck and completely out of their comfort zone as they attempt to go through the usual motions of acting in a play this village has seen hundreds of times already. Parts of it are so bad it's genius and even Steven appears to be enjoying himself.

My own parts are thankfully fairly short. The story more focused on Lady Townsend and her love of Christmas.

Jessy is good at the role. She is probably the most believable in the group, and I can't tear my eyes away when she speaks in her soft voice, her eyes glittering with happiness as she describes Christmas.

Her friend Angie is comical to watch, an impish character who works well with Jessy, and I find myself laughing along with them as they set about preparing the mansion for the Christmas party.

Aside from the odd scenes where I am required to play my part, there is only one I'm focused on and it's up next.

It may be my imagination, but it's as if the tension increases in the room and as I step up to enact my pivotal scene with Jessy, I can almost touch the awkwardness in the air.

We say the lines and as I stare deep into her eyes, I am lost forever.

I lose myself in Jessy. Her vulnerability and the way she smiles tentatively as she battles her nerves. The soft trembling of her rosy red lips and the gentle flush of pink on her face. She is like a vulnerable animal in the hunter's sight, not knowing which way to turn, but somehow transfixed to the spot.

My hand shakes as I reach out and whisper huskily, *"You know it's tradition for a man to catch the woman of his choice under the mistletoe."*

She glances up at the imaginary sprig above our heads and giggles nervously. *"I know that I would be a fool to spurn your advances, my lord, even though the deed has already been done. You captured my heart many years ago and our love has only grown during that time."*

It's as if the entire room is holding its breath as I whisper, *"There has never been another woman for me, my darling Marianne. From the moment I captured you that first time under the mistletoe, it was as if I knew. From that night on, I never looked at anyone else and when you agreed to be my wife, I considered myself the luckiest man alive."*

Jessy's eyes sparkle as I reach out, touching her face

lightly while staring deep into her eyes and I whisper, *"May I steal another kiss, my darling, to strengthen our love?"*

It's as if nobody is watching as she nods, her eyes gleaning under the stage lights that the production crew has rigged up all around the room.

"I will never deny you, my lord." She whispers and as I close the space between us, Morgana yells, "Cut!"

I stop in mid-air and Jessy's eyes widen as reality hits us both hard. For a moment there we were alone in this room. I felt it. We were really going to do this. It was inevitable and more than anything I wanted to kiss her so much it hurts and it was as if Morgana tore my heart out with her words.

"Perfect, darlings. That was amazing. Now, let's move on to the dying scene. Jessy, use the settee as the bed. I mean, obviously we will rig up a proper bed and everything, but for now it will do."

Jessy blinks and then tears her gaze away and forces a smile onto her face.

"Of course."

As I step back, I struggle to get a grip because that was so real. Thank God Morgana stepped in because I was about to make a complete fool of myself because one thing's for sure, every person here would have known of my feelings for her the moment our lips touched.

I take my seat beside Steven, who hands me a glass of mulled wine and chuckles. "You could probably use this, although I'm pretty sure the alcohol burned out with the heat."

"Thanks."

I take a sip and he leans in and whispers, "Morgana did you a favour there."

"How?"

"She prevented an internet sensation when the entire world watched you cheat on her in front of her face."

"Was it that obvious?"

"Pretty much."

"I'm screwed, aren't I?"

"Pretty much."

He chuckles again and then adopts a more serious tone. "Colin is due in the morning now. He's leaving early and wants to get going at ten am."

"It's probably for the best."

I gaze at Jessy lying on the couch while the pretend doctor declares there is no hope and I prepare for my scene when I discover I have lost the only woman I ever loved.

Why does that feel real right now and why does the sense of despair inside me remain even after the alcohol works its magic?

CHAPTER 31
JESSY

The sound of Christmas carols fills the shoppers with Christmas cheer as the cold bite of winter attempts to bring them to their senses. Cinnamon and orange collide in an onslaught to the senses as shops entice you inside with the promise of finding that perfect Christmas gift to tick off your list.

Angie is already several shopping bags in but for some reason I'm lacking inspiration because life has turned on its head and nothing makes sense anymore.

"Hey, Jessy. Do you think my mum will love this scarf?"

I glance across and smile at the vision of Angie with a huge scarf wrapped around her neck several times.

"She will love it." I reply as I stare with frustration at the various candles I've been sniffing for close to five minutes already.

"Hey." Angie appears by my side, concern written in her eyes.

"What's up? You're not really feeling this today, are you?"

"Not really."

She nods towards her crammed basket. "Let me pay for these and we can grab a coffee. I heard their gingerbread cinnamon delight is to die for."

I grab a couple of random candles and line up with her and wonder where my Christmas spirit has gone.

Ordinarily, I love these days with Angie. It's one of the highlights of our year and we save up hard to make it a memorable one. Usually I exhaust my gifting list and head home to wrap the packages in front of a Christmas movie, but I don't even feel like doing that.

It's ever since the 'almost' kiss with Luke. It may be my imagination, but I really sensed a connection between us. The anticipation was high and then Morgana yelled, 'cut' and brought me to my senses. Thank God she did because that could have been the most embarrassing moment of my life and I spent the rest of the evening avoiding Luke, who, in turn, has spent the last few days avoiding me.

I'm aware his physio is taking up most of his time, but there are things I need to run past him regarding the business plan I'm writing. Steven has been the one overseeing that, causing me to wonder if Luke saw the longing in my eyes and was appalled by my infatuation.

It can only be that and so I follow Angie to the coffee shop across the road with a heavy heart and as we manage to grab the last table, I wait for her to order with a heart filled with desolation.

"Here you go."

She sets the steaming coffee before me with a side of shortbread and smiles.

"What's up?"

"I'm sorry, what?"

"You. Ever since the night you *almost* kissed Luke Adams, you've been like a closed book. Did anything happen between you I should know about because I'm seeing a guilty conscience written all over your face?"

"Is it obvious?" I groan and her eyes widen in shock.

"Oh my God! I was joking. You mean you really have done something I should have been told about immediately?"

"Not really. I mean, I haven't done anything. Only inappropriate thoughts concerning my new boss."

"Well, that's hardly a crime, babe. I've had inappropriate thoughts about many men who don't even know I exist. You're just the lucky one who nearly got to act them out."

"In front of his girlfriend, not to mention the village."

I stir my coffee and sigh heavily.

"What am I going to do, Angie? Why do I like him so much knowing he is already taken? What type of person does that make me?"

"Human?"

She leans forward, mischief dancing in her eyes like a candle flame in the wind.

"I admit it's an impossible situation, but there is hope."

"Is there?"

"Of course. I mean, don't forget what I saw that day. Morgana isn't averse to playing away from home either and if I'm right, she is having an illicit affair with Luke's manager, Steven."

"You don't know that? It could have been anything. They are a close group and he could have just been comforting her, or something along those lines."

She stirs her own gingerbread latte with a thoughtful expression.

"Perhaps they are breaking up. You hear about it all the time, couples living a lie. It would explain why he is so keen on you and she is, well, carrying on with his manager."

"I doubt it."

I remember the soft expression in his eyes and the loving way he speaks of her.

"You're just imagining it. Anyway–" I exhale sharply. "As soon as his ankle heals, he'll be heading back to Manchester and Granthaven will be a distant memory."

Angie shrugs. "Possibly, which is why you need to step up your campaign."

"What campaign?"

"Luke, silly. If you are going to stand any chance of winning his heart, you must be ruthless."

I shake my head and make to speak, but she cuts in with an excited, "Take a leaf out of Morgana's book and dress to impress. Show him you are her equal, if not better, and anything she can do you can do too."

"Like what? I'm not becoming an influencer, no way."

"You only need to influence one person, and he is already primed. The play is your perfect chance because if you build the tension and drop subtle hints, when the deed happens, you can all but reel him in."

"You're mad."

The night the mistletoe died

"I'm right and you know it."

She leans back and smiles. "The kiss under the mistletoe is the perfect moment. One taste of your lips and he won't know what hit him."

"If you say so."

I shake my head and concentrate on my latte instead because as plans go, Angie's has all the makings of an unsuccessful one. It will only end with me waving goodbye to him in the New Year while I live with the humiliation of ever thinking a man like Luke would ever be interested in a woman like me.

CHAPTER 32
LUKE

It's been a few days since I last saw Jessy and I'm trying my best to put her out of my mind, but that would be like trying to stop breathing. She fills my thoughts when I'm awake and I dream of her at night. It's as if cupid shot his arrow the moment I stared into her eyes and the poison infected my heart.

I'm making good progress. The boot came off when Colin arrived and he announced my ankle appeared to be fine. A trip to the hospital for an X-ray confirmed his diagnosis, and I have been working it under his careful instructions for the past couple of days.

He leaves today and has left me with a strict set of exercises that I must follow and instructions to head back to the club early in the new year for further physio.

It appears that Christmas is decision time because it's no longer just me to consider anymore and Granthaven's future is decidedly hanging in the balance.

"Luke!"

Morgana calls out and I yell, "I'm in here."

I'm attempting to work out in the room most suited to a potential gym and using the equipment the physio brought with him to strengthen my ankle.

"Hey."

She heads into the room and peers at me with concern. "How's it going?"

"Better than expected." I smile reassuringly, and she sighs with relief.

"That's great, hun. I mean, I love being here and all that, but I'm kind of going stir crazy and want to discuss returning to Manchester in the new year. What are your thoughts on that?"

She perches on a nearby seat and the nerves surrounding her expression don't escape me.

I draw my legs up to the bent position as I regard her carefully.

"It's a difficult decision."

"I get that, hun, but your life is there, at least for the next few years, or even further. Many footballers play in their thirties, and you can't be in two places at once."

"Tell me about it."

She sighs. "I mean, don't get me wrong, this place is kind of magical and it could be amazing with a great deal of money flung at it, but is this your dream, Luke, or is it someone else's?"

"It was *never* my dream, Morgana and I think you know that, but well–"

I gaze out of the window at the serene landscape where the frost is still coating the ground and trees, despite being past lunchtime.

I smile. "But dreams change, priorities change and I'm still working out if that relates to mine."

"I see."

Morgana isn't usually lost for words, but there is obviously something on her mind and she peers around and then heads to the door, closing it carefully.

She heads back and sits beside me, her head finding my shoulder as my arm drapes around her.

"I sense an ending and a new beginning, Luke."

She sounds wistful and I drop a light kiss on the top of her head and my heart hangs heavily inside me.

"We always knew it would happen one day."

"I suppose, but it doesn't make it any easier."

I say nothing because I'm hating this as much as she is and she whispers, "Tell me about Jessy. What are you thinking?"

I allow my mind to wander there and it brings a smile to my face.

"I like her but am conscious it wouldn't work."

"Is that why you've been avoiding her?"

"You noticed then." I chuckle softly, and she turns and kisses me softly on the cheek.

Then she grips my face and turns it to face her and her eyes shine with determination as she says gently, "Sometimes fate throws a curve ball when you least expect it. You have no way of knowing if it will work or not, but you would never forgive yourself if you didn't try at least."

"But how? I mean–" I raise my eyes while I stare at her fondly.

"We're the golden couple, remember, or did you forget when you ventured into the land that time forgot?"

"You know I love you, hun." Her eyes shine with unexpected tears and she whispers, "But I should let you go."

"Are you breaking up with me?"

Something tugs on my heart as we sit huddled on the floor of a mansion that still feels as if I've stepped back in time, as life revolves around us, searching for an exit.

"I suppose I am."

Her fingers find mine and lace them with hers and she says sadly, "I want you to be free to make important choices, Luke. We have reached the end of our road, but will always walk in the same direction. I love you, and I will never forget what you did for me."

My heart is beating way too fast because I'm not sure I'm ready for this. Morgana has been my safety blanket for a long time now and I have hidden behind her willingly, shutting the rest of the world out.

"Have you spoken to Steven?" I ask because I'm interested to hear his thoughts on this, and she smiles.

"Of course, at great length. He was the one who told me of your feelings towards Jessy."

"You mean you didn't pick up on that? You're slipping."

"I've had a lot to deal with, so excuse me for that."

She rolls her eyes and stares around at the room that must have experienced a lot of drama in the past, alongside happiness and great sadness.

"Anyway–" She huffs. "Steven said it was the perfect time to make the change. My business is established, so thank you for that."

She grins and I chuckle. "You're welcome."

She squeezes my hand. "Plus, both of us are tired of

hiding our relationship. It worked all the time we were building something, but I kind of love the guy and want the world to know that. It's time for us to consider our position and start building our life – together."

She peers at me with concern. "But not unless you're happy. I want you to be happy more than anything and somehow I think Jessy is the answer to that."

"I do love you, baby."

I drop a light kiss on her forehead and she smiles. "And I love you too and I always will, but it's time, Luke and I have the perfect plan to make all our dreams come true."

Before I can ask what that is, the door opens and I'm surprised to see Jessy standing awkwardly in the doorway, looking so embarrassed as she sees us huddled together on the floor.

"Oh, I'm sorry – I'll–"

"Jessy, babe, come in. It's fine. I was just leaving."

"But, I'm well, I don't want to interrupt–"

She makes to leave and Morgana nudges me and I say loudly, "Jessy, wait."

She stops and I draw in a huge breath and say firmly, "We should catch up. Meet me in the kitchen. I'd love a coffee and I think you would too."

"Well, um, if you're sure."

"I'm sure."

Morgana jumps up and rubs the dust from her leggings and sighs.

"Honestly, Luke. I thought we had dealt with the dust problem, but we must have missed this room."

She peers around and shakes her head. "I'll find

Jasper. We're filming today anyway and we need you after lunch, so make sure you're dressed appropriately."

I'm guessing my sweat-drenched sweatpants and T-shirt won't cut it for the camera, and I shrug. "Of course. What's the plan?"

"Christmas shopping, of course." She winks as I groan. "You'll love it and imagine the photos on my feed, plus I'm doing a vlog later and would appreciate your participation. It's been a while and my subscribers are asking."

She nods to Jessy.

"Hey, why don't you come with us? You must know all the best places for a great photo opportunity and I could use some help. What about dinner out, too? It will be so much fun."

Jessy hesitates and I catch her eye and smile. "Please, Jessy. Morgana's right, we could all use a night off, and I would love for you to join us."

Morgana rolls her eyes, but Jessy can't see that and I understand what she's annoyed about. In one practised sentence, I've relegated Jessy to the third wheel, which is the exact opposite of what Morgana is planning.

Jessy nods but I note the awkwardness in her smile as she says lightly, "That's great. I'll – um – well, I'll put the kettle on and meet you both in the kitchen while you, well, finish up here."

She bolts away like a startled fawn and Morgana sighs.

"Honestly, Luke, you may as well have snogged me in front of her, the poor woman."

"I don't understand. Why would Jessy care?"

I'm confused and Morgana's eyes sparkle with

mischief as she whispers, "Because that woman is so in love with you, and you're the idiot who can't see it."

She heads out of the room, shaking her head, leaving me staring after her with a bemused expression on my face. Jessy doesn't love me. Morgana is very wrong about that and yet, if it's true, it changes everything.

CHAPTER 33
JESSY

I feel bad. I barged into their private moment, and even though they were nice about it I hurt inside. It's obvious they are just nice people and any thoughts that Luke regards me any differently are firmly in my imagination.

As I wait for them to join me, I attempt to reign in my emotions, feelings, and desires and view him as my boss. My amazing, gorgeous, sweet, kind, and sexy boss.

I groan inside because how will this work? I am an idiot. A self-obsessed deluded idiot who should really start hunting for a proper job as soon as possible. Preferably a woman boss and far away from men like Luke Adams. Far away from a television even because he is sure to feature on Match of The Day on a weekly basis.

"Jessy."

He heads inside the kitchen, running his fingers through his dishevelled hair and flashes the lopsided grin that catches my heart every single time.

"I'm glad you stopped by."

I say nothing because he is probably only being polite, anyway.

He flicks the switch on the kettle and glances around the room.

"This place would be great with a modern kitchen. I wonder how much it would cost?"

"A lot." I shrug and try hard to prevent my heart from beating too fast as I contemplate a decision may have been made. Surely he wouldn't be picturing the interior if he intends on heading back to Manchester in the new year.

It brings me back to the reason I came here in the first place, and I set my notebook down on the kitchen counter.

"I've been working on the business plan."

"Great."

He selects two mugs from the draining board and I glance towards the door. "I thought Morgana was joining us."

"No, she has a meeting with Jasper. They are organising more filming and I wish I wasn't involved, but they need me, apparently."

He grimaces, making me smile.

"So, you're not a fan of being on camera. Perhaps you can sympathise with Scott."

"I totally sympathise with Scott but my life dictates I must grin and bear it."

He holds up the mug. "Sugar?"

"No, thanks."

He hands me the coffee and nods towards the notebook.

"I'm interested in hearing your business plan."

"Are you?"

I raise my eyes and he grins sheepishly. "Well, maybe not dying to hear it, but it's probably going to help with my decision."

"Have you made it yet?" I'm curious, and he shakes his head and exhales sharply. "Not yet, but let's just say it's work in progress. Anyway, run it past me, and I'll add it to the long list of things I need to think of before the new year."

We spend the next two hours drinking coffee and discussing the business plan and I must admit it is nice to be sitting side by side sharing information and attempting to figure a way out of his mess.

Luke

We are interrupted when Morgana and Steven head into the room, Jasper, as always, in tow and Morgana says happily, "Come on, guys. We're heading to Dorchester to grab some festive atmosphere and Jasper and the crew will film some great scenes for the show."

I sigh heavily and smile my apology to Jessy who appears lost for words and I'm guessing it's due to the fact Morgana resembles a polar bear in a white fur hat, matching coat and boots, with skin tight red velvet leggings that match her painted lips.

"I'd better change." I say quickly, knowing my own exercise gear won't make the final cut, and Morgana groans with exasperation. "Honestly, Luke, I told you about this two hours ago. What on earth have you been doing?"

She doesn't even wait for a reply before she says over

her shoulder as she heads to the door, "You'll have to meet us there. Jessy can drive you, and I'll text our location. See you soon."

We watch the group leave and Jessy says quickly, "I'm so sorry, I've taken up too much of your time. I'll drop you there and leave you to it."

"Oh no you don't." I groan loudly. "If I'm spending the afternoon from hell Christmas shopping, I'm taking you with me."

I wink, causing her to blush adorably and nod towards the kettle. "Make yourself another coffee if you like. I won't be long."

As I head out of the room, for the first time since coming here, it's as if something has shifted inside me and I view this place differently. My conversation with Morgana earlier appears to have been the catalyst to drive change, and now it's up to me to steer it in the right direction.

∽

"Is it far?" I ask as we set off from Granthaven Manor in Jessy's small car and she shakes her head. "No. About twenty minutes."

She peers at my foot that is without its boot.

"How's your ankle?"

"Good thanks. You know, I was a little worried back there. I kind of need my limbs to be working to do my job."

"How long before you can – do your job, I mean?"

I shrug. "A few weeks, maximum."

"I see." She falls silent and so do I because we are

both aware that my job is nowhere near Granthaven and it prompts me to say carefully, "I expect you're wondering where that leaves you?"

Her cheeks are pink as she says nervously, "A little, and the village, of course."

"Of course."

I gaze out of the window at the passing hedgerows and once again it strikes me how beautiful the countryside is around here, prompting me to ask, "What are your plans, Jessy? Your hopes and dreams. You must have them."

"I do."

She clears her throat and says in a small voice, "More than anything, I want to be happy and if that means moving on and finding my dream outside of Granthaven, then I must accept that."

"But you love this place?"

"I do, but I'm also aware that things don't stay the same forever. You see–"

She shifts the gear, and the car climbs up a steep hill and she says over the screaming engine, "I've also experienced life outside Granthaven and discovered it's not as scary as I thought it was. Life goes on and it's what you make of it, wherever you happen to be at the time. When I returned home, everything looked different somehow. I saw its faults as well as the beauty of the place, and it made me wonder if I had grown away from it."

"You want to leave?"

My heart sinks because I don't want Jessy to have any desire to leave this place, and she nods. "I do. You see, Luke, I want to experience the wonder of the world. Granthaven is a speck of happiness in that amazing world that I know so little of. I want to visit places I have only read about and experience nature in all its forms."

"I see."

I don't know why I hate every word she speaks. I suppose because it shows she isn't thinking of me and it hurts. Jessy's dreams and wishes involve travel and I must face the fact I've lost her before she even realises that I found her.

CHAPTER 34
JESSY

I am trying so hard to distance myself from this man. I have a job to do which is all that should concern me because it's obvious he is in love with his girlfriend. I shouldn't be having any thoughts about him other than he's my boss and from now on, that is exactly how I'm going to view him. He's my boss for however long we have and I must consider my future without him in it.

His company is relaxed and it would be so easy to be on more familiar terms. He acts more like a friend than a boss and I suppose that's why I'm struggling. But I must try to draw the invisible line between us if I'm to survive with my sanity intact, so I keep my cool and act polite but show none of the interest I'm feeling inside.

He makes polite conversation on the way to Dorchester and I spin some tale about wanting to travel. I don't, really. Obviously, I want to go on holidays and experience other cultures, but more than anything I want to settle down and build a life with someone I love and who loves me in return.

I want the dream I've held since I was a child, even before I understood what dreams were. Aside from the castle and the golden carriage, of course. Even I had to draw the line somewhere.

My parents have a happy marriage. They set the bar high and even though they never had much money, we never felt that as children. Both my sister and I had a happy childhood and now I want to offer the same to my children.

But I keep it all to myself because Luke Adams definitely doesn't need to know that.

∼

We park in the main carpark and Luke groans. "I hate Christmas shopping."

I laugh. "And I expect you do that a lot because—"

He grins, causing that ache in my heart that just won't go away.

"Not really, but I can hate the thought of it, can't I?"

"If you say so."

I roll my eyes and make to pay for the parking at the machine and Luke's hand covers mind, causing me to jump. "I'll get this."

His soft expression as he stares into my eyes causes my heart to race faster and once again we share a moment because I couldn't tear my eyes away if I tried.

"Are you Luke Adams?" A young voice interrupts and Luke drags his eyes away from mine to a boy staring at him hopefully.

"Yes." Luke smiles, turning his charm on the small boy who adds, "Your team is rubbish. I support Arsenal."

"Ouch."

Luke pretends to stagger and the boy laughs. "You're okay though. Have you ever thought about transferring to Arsenal? They may be interested if you get your ankle fixed."

I suppress the giggle that isn't far away because you can always rely on children to say it how it is.

"Do you think they'd have me?" Luke replies good-naturedly and the boy shrugs. "Who knows? They may be interested."

He says hopefully, "I don't suppose you could take our photo?"

He is looking at me and I smile. "Of course, if it's okay with Luke."

"Sure." He says and as the boy hands me his phone, I snap several and hand it back to his eager hands.

"That will annoy Ben Stevens."

"Who is he?" Luke asks and the boy grins.

"Probably the only boy in the school who supports the Rangers."

"The only one?"

Luke is shocked and the boy nods. "We're mainly Arsenal supporters mixed with a few Southampton ones, but as their team is rubbish too, they keep quiet about it."

His mother calls and he shouts, "Coming!" and then casts an appreciative smile in Luke's direction and holds up his phone. "You're cool though. Happy Christmas."

"Same to you."

We watch the boy bound over to his mother, who appears to be telling him off, probably for talking to strangers. Then I see her do a double-take and her attitude changes in a heartbeat, so I say quickly, "Come on, let's pay before you get swamped."

"I doubt it." Luke rolls his eyes. "It appears the whole of Dorset supports Arsenal anyway, so if I get to experience anything, it's probably them running me out of town."

He pays for the ticket and as I place it on my dashboard, I shiver as the icy wind curls around any exposed part of my flesh.

I'm surprised when Luke unwraps the Burberry scarf from around his neck and before I can say anything, winds it around mine with a sweet smile.

"Here, allow me."

"But–"

He shakes his head. "No buts. I don't want to be responsible for you catching a cold. Who would I kiss under the mistletoe then?"

My face must be flaming and I say quickly, "So it's self-preservation, so you don't have to catch my germs. Is that what you're saying?"

He shrugs. "I may have already caught something. That's the trouble with things you can't see. You don't know when they hit you."

For some reason, I don't think he's talking about germs and as the scarf nestles around my neck, I can smell his aftershave and still feel the heat from his body.

I am so conflicted, my emotions in overdrive and as we head towards the shopping centre, I wish more than anything we were here as a couple and not one half of another one.

Morgana texts Luke her location, and we head to the

nearby pub to meet up with them. As we head inside, I notice her immediately, surrounded by fellow shoppers, all keen on taking selfies with her.

Luke laughs softly. "She's so good at that."

I must admit she is and I doubt there is a person in this pub who isn't mesmerised by the star in their midst.

She waves and all heads turn our way as she yells, "Luke, honey, come over here and bring Jessy with you."

Luke nods and whispers, "I'm sorry, Jessy. It's always a bit of a circus when you go out in public with Morgana."

I guess she's only half the attraction and once again, my heart sinks. I don't belong in their world as a paid employee or otherwise. I should give up on even praying for a Christmas miracle because I really don't stand a chance.

I edge in beside Jasper, who is studying the photographs on his phone, a half empty glass of lager in front of him and he says without taking his eyes off the screen, "Hey, babe. Tell the barman what you want. We're running a tab."

The fact the bar is now several feet away, between which is a huddle of mainly women, all desperately trying to get to Morgana, makes my heart sink.

"I'm good, thanks."

Steven leans across on my other side and pushes a glass of wine in my direction.

"Have Morgana's. She hasn't touched it yet; she hasn't had the chance and I'll weather the storm and grab her another."

"But I'm driving." I remind him and he huffs, "Of course. Never mind, I'll fetch it for you instead. What do you want?"

"Just an orange juice, thanks."

I smile as Luke glances my way, a huge smile on his face as he poses with Morgana and a couple of young women, and I note the adoration on their faces, and not just for him. Luke and Morgana are considered a power couple and she deserves the recognition for their success even more than Luke because she relentlessly creates content, while making sure she looks good and tries extra hard to make everyone feel good about themselves.

As I watch them together, smiling and laughing, his arm around her shoulders, tossing loving glances her way, I admit defeat.

Angie is wrong. I can't possibly compete with that.

CHAPTER 35
LUKE

This is why I never go out. It always descends into chaos, and we achieve nothing. I understand this is Morgana's lifeblood. The sheer number of photos will be re-posted on her fan's feeds and attract even more followers to the woman herself.

I still can't believe how much money she makes from this business, as well as the opportunities that pour in from advertising deals and appearance fees. She is offered holidays, clothing, jewellery and experiences, to name but a few. All she must do is one post about how much she likes something and she charges in excess of ten thousand pounds for them. Morgana is wealthy in her own right and equally as famous as me, and I was there at the beginning.

I note Steven pushing his way to the bar and my heart softens. It was his idea. Morgana and Steven have been dating for well over two years and she was a struggling influencer back then. They met at a party where she was one of the paid models and the rest is history.

It was his idea to raise her profile by making her my fake girlfriend. It suited me because I was single and the target of many women, all desperate to be the next wag and it was a nightmare. The club were angry about the endless stories of me in the press, 'the player off the field' was the usual headline as I was pictured with a different woman every night. They always made it look as if it was more than just a selfie request and it was a huge problem.

Steven was concerned because a few of the girls inferred we'd shared more than a photograph and he was concerned I would be the target of a smear campaign, or worse. So Luke and Morgana were born out of a shared interest and I wasn't lying, I do love her, but not in a romantic way.

The three of us are best friends and now we have a different problem entirely because I appear to have fallen for the one woman who has made me look twice and away from the game and I'm unsure what to do about that.

I can't tell her. She may not feel the same way and my breakup with Morgana must be managed skilfully.

We can't have pictures of me cheating on her, just as she is careful to keep her relationship with Steven behind closed doors.

It's an impossible situation and coupled with the inheritance and my injury, I have a great deal on my mind and no answers.

We finally manage to work our way through the crowds and as I take my seat beside Morgana, she whispers, "So, how did it go? I've been dying to ask."

"How did what go?"

I'm genuinely confused, and she nudges me sharply. "With Jessy, of course."

She peers across the table at the woman who is trying to remain invisible right now and looks so miserable I feel responsible.

"She isn't interested."

"And you know this because–" Morgana reminds me that she never takes anything on face value and I whisper back, "I asked what she wanted in life and she told me it was to travel. She wants to leave Granthaven and do better and I got the impression she wants to do it alone."

"You got the impression."

Morgana rolls her eyes. "Honestly, Luke, impressions aren't facts. You really are hopeless, you know."

She smiles as Steven places another round of drinks on the table and she jerks her head in my direction.

"Take this one shopping, Steven, and make him buy gifts for everyone he knows."

"You're seriously asking me to be responsible for that."

Steven chuckles and Morgana shrugs. "I trust in you babe, and don't forget yours truly. You know what I like."

She fastens her gaze on Jessy's small figure wrapped tightly inside my scarf and smiles. "I'll take Jessy with me. Jasper wants to shop alone; he already told me that and so I suggest that in two hours' time, we meet back here to return to the manor house."

"Two hours!"

Steven and I speak at the same time, both of us horrified at that amount of time, and she shrugs. "If you're early, have another drink. It's no hardship."

She glances across at Jessy and says loudly, "Jessy,

hun, will you take pity on me and show me around the town? I really must grab some gifts because time is running out."

Jessy nods. "No problem."

She smiles and once again something strikes me hard in the heart and I suppose this is the moment I accept that without any question, I am falling in love with Jessy Potter and there is absolutely nothing I can do about it.

~

"This is a disaster! Where's the department store?"

Steven grumbles as we wander around a town that appears to be made up of shops that I've never heard of.

Steven is equally lost and groans. "I was certain they'd be a John Lewis or Selfridges here and we could find the personal shopper, give them our list and wait in the restaurant."

"Same."

I shiver against the cold wind and stare miserably at the lit doorways, crammed with shoppers who are all in an apparent feeding frenzy as they grab their last-minute purchases in a state of panic.

I'm no different and then nudge Steven when I spy Jasper looking very pleased with himself, armed with a multitude of bags as he peers into a nearby shop window.

"Leave this to me." I say with determination and we head across to him, making him jump as I slap him on the back.

"Oh, guys, it's you. I thought I was being mugged." He holds a hand to his heart and breathes deeply.

"You are." I grin. "You are obviously a professional

shopper, Jasper, and we are not. What do you say if we relieve you of these and head back to the pub, leaving you with our credit cards and our lists, plus a hefty personal shopping fee for your trouble?"

Jasper's face breaks out into an excited smile. "Wow, I'd do it for free. I adore shopping."

He thrusts the packages in our arms and then holds out his hand for the cards and the list.

Steven grins as we both rattle off what we need - recipient wise and Jasper nods with a serious expression. "Leave it with me guys. Consider me your Christmas shopping fairy."

He rushes off, almost squealing in anticipation and as we head back to the warm and cosy pub, Steven laughs. "Ingenious."

"You're welcome."

Once we are firmly stationed back in our seats in front of the roaring fire, Steven whispers, "Morgana told me about your conversation."

"What do you think?"

I'm anxious because Steven is part of this too.

"That it was always going to happen."

"I suppose."

He appears thoughtful.

"It may have come at the right time."

"In what way?"

"Well, a lot is happening right now and you have some life-changing decisions to make."

He wraps his hand around his pint glass and sighs. "As I see it, you have a few choices. The first is that you decided to relocate to Granthaven and Morgana wasn't happy about that and you split due to a conflict of interests. That you were growing apart anyway, and it was a natural break with no hard feelings on either side."

"And if I don't want to relocate and give up everything I've worked so hard for?"

"That you have grown apart and your trip here merely reinforced that, leaving you both mutually agreeing to separate in the new year. That you will always be friends, but nothing more."

"Then what happens when Morgana is pictured with you and the press makes out she cheated on me? You know they will because it's what they do to sell their fake news."

"Says the man who's made it his business to spread his own fake news."

Steven chuckles softly.

"We're all in this together, Steven. Remember that." I groan. "This is going to break the internet."

I'm aware how many thousands of people are invested in my relationship with Morgana, and it would be as if they were breaking up along with us. We obviously never thought this through properly because it's not just a case of posting a joint announcement and getting on with our lives. There will be the rumours, the conspiracy theories, the blame and the accusations. It will be like a messy divorce played out in the most bitter of ways.

"Or we could do nothing at all until it becomes a problem."

Steven smiles reassuringly. "You have a lot on your mind right now and really don't need another problem to deal with. Let's get Christmas over with and see where we're at in the new year."

"I'm glad you said that, man, because the other option was giving me a headache."

I note a couple of women huddled together in the corner, giggling and staring my way, and I smile as one of them is trying to take photographs by pretending she's taking a selfie. I've seen it all before and it doesn't matter to me. I'm happy to provide a photograph, but it merely reminds me how vulnerable I am regarding posts online. Morgana has always been the firewall between me and scandal, and now as I prepare to knock it down, I realise I'm a lot safer where I am.

CHAPTER 36
JESSY

The wind may be cold but the atmosphere is very warm as I experience shopping with a woman who sets the internet alight. We are stopped constantly by women wanting a selfie with her and gushing over how much they love her vlogs and envy her relationship with Luke Adams.

Every word is like a knife to my heart because it reminds me I am no competition at all. Not that I should even be thinking of her boyfriend, because he is Morgana's and I'm not *that girl*. I never imagined I was, but there is something about Luke that speaks to my soul.

We finally make it into a shop, and as we move around it, Morgana sweeps several items into her basket with no consideration.

She grins as she adds a designer aftershave set and whispers, "Shopping is my greatest skill, Jessy. I know exactly what my friends and family will like and have it all mapped out in my head beforehand."

She points to a well-known brand of aftershave and

says with a smile of triumph, "This is Luke's favourite. I mean, he's so difficult to buy for because he has everything, but he gets through that stuff as if he bathes in it."

She selects the largest one and adds a body lotion and aftershave balm to the mix.

"Steven prefers this one." She lifts another well-known brand from the shelf and adds several other products into her basket and then whispers, "Stocking fillers. I have some great activity gifts already lined up."

"Activity?"

This is so interesting, and she nods, obviously very pleased with herself.

"Well, Luke is a speed freak and loves nothing more than racing car experiences or skiing down the black run. So, for him, I've arranged grid tickets and a personal invitation from Mercedes to join their hospitality at the next Silverstone Grand Prix. He will be able to soak up the atmosphere on the grid and meet his heroes and then watch the race from the garage. It's truly an amazing experience."

I stare at her in awe because what the hell happened to giving someone a pair of socks for Christmas?

She carries on. "Steven loves collecting sporting memorabilia, and I managed to secure David Beckham's number seven jersey when he won the treble with Manchester United. It's signed and dated and everything. He'll be so happy."

She smiles warmly. "I love gifting, Jessy. It's a pleasure to see the happiness it brings, but nothing makes me happier than spending time with my loved ones. That's the best gift ever."

"I agree."

I smile, picturing my own family unwrapping their gifts at Christmas and the chaos that brings with it.

"What about you, hun, is there anyone special on your Christmas gift list?"

Her question only reinforces how alone I am, and I smile to disguise how much that bothers me.

"Just family and friends, of course."

"So, there's no guy."

"No, just me."

"What about that Scott guy who was going to play the lord?"

I shake my head vigorously. "No, Scott is like my brother. Even the idea of that is wrong?"

"I take your point." She grins. "Is there anyone you have your eye on?"

"No."

My face is heated as I lift a beautiful necklace off a nearby stand and admire it, hoping to distract my guilt away from the only man who interests me and she gasps, "I love that necklace. You should really get that, if not for a gift, for yourself. It matches your eyes."

I note the hefty price tag and replace it carefully. "Maybe in the sales."

I'm aware of Morgana's overflowing basket, whereas mine has a box of my mum's favourite chocolates and a book on walks in the Dorset countryside for Dad. Nothing even remotely as expensive or desirable as Morgana's choices, which once again reflect how far apart we really are.

As we pay, Morgana spends her time in the line skilfully balancing her basket and her phone as she records something on it for her vlog and once we have paid and spill out onto the street, she says happily, "So, Jessy. What are your plans for the new year?"

"I'm not sure."

I'm nervous even considering that and I suppose it's because I may not have a job if Luke decides Granthaven isn't for him and heads back to the city.

Morgana nods as if she understands every thought in my head and I only hope to God that isn't the case, because then her smile would turn to a scowl quicker than David Beckham could curl one into the net from a free kick.

The selfie she snaps of us makes me feel even worse because she looks like a Christmas ad with her white fur and bright smile, while I'm just the awkward one in my red bobble hat and boring coat.

Come to think of it, Angie wasn't wrong when she said I should shape up in that department. Spending time with Morgana only illustrates how far I've let myself go, and once again that doesn't make me feel any better at all.

"What about Luke?"

It's as if she slapped me around the face and I stutter, "Luke, um, I don't understand."

"What do you think of him?"

I am lost for words because there is so much I can say to describe him. The soft kind smiles he directs my way. The twinkle in his eye and the consideration he shows when I'm around. His gentle humour and desire to do the right thing, not to mention his astonishing good looks and amazing body. He is the whole package and I'm still searching for his faults because I have yet to discover any. He is the perfect man, for me anyway, and Morgana is the luckiest woman alive.

She doesn't wait for an answer and says with a soft smile. "You like him, don't you?"

I am now incredibly hot and gasp, "Only in a friend, boss, stroke employee way, of course."

"It's okay, Jessy, it's perfectly fine if you do."

The conversation I had with Angie is biting hard right now as I consider Morgana and Luke in an open relationship, and I shift awkwardly on the spot.

Morgana leans closer and glances around before she says in a low voice, "Keep this to yourself but Luke and I – well–"

"Oh my God, it's Morgana!"

A shriek, high-pitched yell almost deafens me as a group of young girls stampede in our direction and Morgana straightens up and paints a broad smile on her face.

"Hey girls."

I watch as they squeal their delight and pose for several photographs with the gorgeous influencer and ask her many questions that she answers with good grace. They say a crowd attracts a crowd and we are soon ten deep in delighted euphoria as the crowd grows while she attempts to keep everyone happy. I have my work cut out holding her bags and acting as some kind of security and wondering how she puts up with it at all.

It's only when she says loudly, "Sorry guys, it's bloody freezing out here. I must run, but remember to check out my Christmas vlog. There will be some coupon codes on there that you won't want to miss."

She blows kisses to her adoring public and as we head off, I'm left wondering what she was about to tell me before we were so rudely interrupted.

CHAPTER 37
LUKE

It's been one week since we shopped in Dorchester and I last saw Jessy.

When she dropped me back to the manor, she appeared distracted and refused my invitation to come inside, citing a prior engagement.

We have been caught in our own agendas ever since and while Jessy works on the business plan for Granthaven, I have been working on my fitness so I can return to the only thing I know — football.

Morgana and Jasper have been concentrating on the show and Steven has been liaising between me and the club and organising my diary, which he excels at.

He isn't just my agent, he's a good friend and is the first point of contact for anyone wishing to book me for events, sponsorships and general enquiries and we get a lot of those.

Before my ankle snapped, I was the top goalscorer at Manchester Rangers and there were several clubs all bidding for me in the January transfer window. Arsenal included. That amuses me because I'm guessing I would be more popular around here and yet I have no desire to leave the club I supported as a boy. I am living my dream, but as is often with dreams, they can change into a nightmare just as quickly.

"Hey."

Morgana heads into the kitchen, where I'm taking a break, and smiles. "How are you, hun?"

"I'm good, thanks. What about you?"

"It's all good. Tonight we're hosting the village carol evening where they will assemble in the hallway and we will hand out cookies and mulled wine as we listen to their angelic choir."

I raise my eyes and she grins. "Trust me, it will be so wholesome and make the most amazing segment in the show."

"How's that coming along?"

Aside from the odd time I'm required to talk on camera, this is Morgana's show, and she is putting one hundred per cent of her efforts into it. The house itself has been transformed in a very short time, courtesy of the production crew and it is tasteful, homely and screams Christmas.

There is the huge tree that sparkles in the hallway, reflected in the various mirrors she has placed there. The wood panelling gleams and the air is scented with cinnamon and pine cones, the huge swag decorating the giant staircase being a particular triumph. The fire burns in the woodburner, creating a warm welcome and the rooms off from it are equally good.

Jasper really knows his stuff, and I continually remind myself that this is all a film set. It will be torn down as quickly as it went up, but it allows me to imagine what it could be like with a lot of money and vision spent on it.

"Have you seen Jessy?" Morgana asks, and I shake my head.

"No. I think she's avoiding me."

I remind myself of the many texts I've sent her, checking if she needs anything more as an excuse for communication than anything. She is always polite but keeps it formal and my heart sinks when I realise I'm not very good at this. It's why I'm still single, I suppose, and readily accepted Steven's plan to pretend to be Morgana's boyfriend. It suited me – suited us and yet now it doesn't suit me at all.

I want to be free.

"She's coming tonight. Angie told me they would both be here. In fact, in her words, they wouldn't miss it for the world."

"What am I going to do, Morgana?"

I sigh. "This is an impossible situation. How can I show any interest in Jessy without coming clean about our arrangement?"

"It will all work out."

She tries to reassure me, but I'm not so sure.

"You see, it's probably best if we let things ride as they are because the new year is uncertain."

She's not wrong there and as I drain the last dregs of my coffee, I face the prospect of an afternoon concentrating on my fitness.

As I make to leave, Morgana reminds me, "Make yourself Christmas carol ready at six, Luke. The producers want it in one take if possible."

As I leave the room, it strikes me that nothing in my

life is real. Even Christmas is being staged and if the public knew just how far we have gone, I doubt they would be impressed.

Smoke and mirrors. That is exactly what we live by, and I don't want to do it anymore.

The show, the girlfriend and this house, are all make believe and I already know that when I return to Manchester, life will carry on as before. I will perform and go through the motions of acting a part and outwardly I have everything. Inwardly, I am empty and severely lacking of substance and in my mind the only person who can save me from that is the one woman I can't stop thinking about.

∞

As REQUESTED, I head downstairs at six pm and find the hallway full of the crew, running around, rigging up lighting and testing camera angles. Morgana is dressed in red velvet leggings this time, with a Christmas sweater with her hair curled to her shoulders, her make-up perfect and her lips painted red. She also smells amazing and her brilliant white smile welcomes me as I push through the crowd towards her.

"Luke, darling." She grabs my hand and her eyes sparkle. "This is going to be epic. I can't wait to open the door to Christmas."

I raise my brow and she giggles. "That's the title Jasper wants to name the episode. Opening the door to Christmas."

She appears so animated I smile and she whispers above the general hum, "The carollers will be provided with an old-fashioned lantern and a book of carols. Their feet will crunch under the gravel as they crowd around the front door, the potted trees on either side glowing with the soft warm ambiance of fairy lights. The giant wreath on the door will also be lit and as the chief caroller, the one who holds the donation bucket, Mr Spalding, I'm guessing–" She shrugs. "Anyway, he will knock loudly on the door and we will open it as a team and gasp in delight at the pure vision of wholesome innocence before us."

My heart sinks. What the hell!

She has a dreamy expression on her face as she whispers reverently, "We will stand together with your arm draped over my shoulder. I'll have tears in my eyes as we listen to the heavenly angelic tones of the villagers. As they serenade us with their voices, we will gaze fondly into one another's eyes and offer a gentle, loving smile as we turn to smile our appreciation for their efforts."

I take a deep calming breath as she gasps, "Then, when they finish, I will invite them in for an encore around the amazing tree, the shot firmly focused on the door opening into a Christmas paradise with the tree at the centre of the shot."

"Morgana – I –"

She carries on relentlessly.

"As the fire roars its welcome and the tree lights sparkle, there will be beautifully wrapped gifts under the tree, colour coordinated, of course. The scent of warm mince pies and mulled wine will permeate the air and when the carollers cease singing soft old-fashioned Christmas tunes, Nat King Cole will play softly in the background of the merry excited chatter."

Before I can even express my dubious opinion on this, Jasper rushes in and shouts, "Places everyone! The villagers are heading this way and I need Sasha and Adrian outside pronto to distribute the lanterns and carol sheets."

Morgana claps her hands with excitement and I don't have the heart to ruin her carefully contrived moment, but to be honest, this is the last thing I want to do and pray for a Christmas miracle to spare my disbelieving heart.

CHAPTER 38
JESSY

Angie is almost quivering with excitement as we follow the huddle of villagers towards Granthaven Manor. We are dressed in bobble hats and gloves, our thick coats attempting to shelter us from the elements.

The stars are out in force tonight and the crisp frosty air makes my teeth chatter, despite the hand warmers I shoved into my gloves.

I wish I had some for my boots because my feet are groaning in protest as the ice pinches my toes and my breath escapes like mist into the icy cold air.

"It's not like Vienna, is it love?" Mum grumbles, as she clings onto dad's gloved hand and he growls, "I'm missing Mission Impossible three for this."

"That you can watch on catch up." Mum reminds him.

"Don't be such a grinch."

Angie's parents aren't far behind and I hear Margery

grumble, "I gave up bingo for this debacle. The mince pies better be good."

"Attention everyone!" Mr Spalding calls from his position at the head of the procession. "Remember, we are representing Granthaven on the world stage. Please rest your voices and set them free when they are needed."

"Miserable old sod." Wilf growls a few feet in front of us and Angie nudges me and whispers, "I'm not sure the gun is considered a festive prop."

She giggles as we stare at the incongruous sight of Wilf striding toward the manor house dressed in his usual wax jacket and woolly hat.

I note several familiar faces, all wishing they were anywhere else, but Mr Spalding assured us it was necessary to raise awareness of the village plight. If we can attract sponsorship or donations to the regeneration of the land that time forgot, it would be in all our best interests as the founder members of Granthaven. Personally, I think he's backing a loser because I'm aware of how many millions we need and it will take a lot more than a seemingly impromptu carol concert to raise that amount of money.

Angie gasps as we notice the blazing torches lining our way and the lake lit by floodlights that project lifelike snowflakes that dance across the surface.

"Wow!"

Angie gasps and mum says in awe, "This is amazing. I've never seen anything like it."

Knowing Morgana, I wouldn't be surprised to see ice skating penguins doing the Bolero on the frozen lake, such is the power of movie magic and I note the camera men lining the route as we march up to the house.

As we pass through the torches, we are handed an old-fashioned lantern by a member of the production team who is dressed in black to blend into the shadows, along with a carol sheet for good measure.

Angie gets a fit of the giggles as she whispers, "Are they aware that none of us can sing?"

I laugh. "They soon will be."

As we near the great door, I admire the amazing wreath that is lit on the freshly painted wood and stare at the fairy lights in the potted trees with envy. This is exactly how I imagined the manor house would look in its glory days and I must hand it to Morgana and Jasper, they certainly know their stuff.

Mr Spalding knocks loudly on the door as we gather around in a huddle, our lanterns raised, while we try hard to appear happy to be here.

As the door swings open, he acts like a conductor and begins to sing Silent Night in his best Alfie Boe's voice.

The rest of us frantically search for the words, holding the lanterns up to find them and after an awkward start, we attempt to join in. I say attempt because half of the carollers can't even see the words and are relying on memory to get them through each verse.

I peer past Wilf and notice Luke standing in the doorway and my breath catches when I register his arm around Morgana, who simply looks amazing. She definitely deserves her celebrity status because she exudes glamour and the fond twinkle in his eye lights the darkness as he gazes at her lovingly.

The words to the song stick in my throat and my misery is compounded when she impulsively leans up and kisses him softly on the lips. I can only imagine the cameras catching the tender moment for posterity and if I had a white flag, I would raise it now.

Luke will never be mine.

It's obvious, and I'm the idiot who truly believed he could be.

Silent night turns to Hallelujah and I swear even the birds head for cover. Wilf is drowning everyone out with his own rendition and Mr Spalding is throwing murderous glances his way as he attempts to sing over him. Angie gets another fit of the giggles as Harriet Haughton shrieks like a banshee and as carollers go, we definitely don't deserve the title.

I steal a glance at the happy couple and note Morgana's happy smile is a little startled now and Luke appears to be struggling to maintain a straight face.

It's obviously a disaster and I can't help myself as I dissolve into giggles along with Angie, who is laughing so hard her lantern is wobbling.

Mum hisses, "Girls, please remember the cameras. Pull yourselves together."

Angie does that snorting thing, which even makes mum laugh out loud.

"Cut! Cut!"

We are saved as Jasper waves his hands in the air and claps his hands. "Thank you everyone. Maybe we should move inside now."

We don't need to be asked twice and collectively surge for the door and as we enter the lit hallway, Angie gasps, "It's beautiful!"

For once we are all stunned into silence as we take in the glorious tree that rises majestically from the ground up, the beautiful star on the top twinkling like the Star of Bethlehem.

A collective 'ooh' echoes around the room and Jasper says loudly from his position of great height on the staircase, "Okay, now let's try that again from hymn number four. The Holly and The Ivy."

As the music plays through the speakers, I notice the words are being sung for us, meaning none of us are required to do anything other than mouth them. Although some do try. It's like religious karaoke as we follow along, belting out the words and hoping this is over quickly and the mulled wine makes an appearance.

One hour later, we are all a little disgruntled, but it appears that Jasper is in a happier mood and as he calls 'cut' there's a gentle murmur of relief from the dozens of villagers who turned out for a free glass of wine accompanied by a mince pie and the chance to see how the other half live.

Luke and Morgana are handing out the aforementioned delicacies and I attempt to hide behind dad when Luke heads our way armed with a silver tray.

As he offers dad a mulled wine, he peers behind him and grins.

"There she is."

Dad shifts and shakes his head. "What are you doing hiding back there, Jessy?"

Mum glances between us and smirks, and my face burns as I pretend that I wasn't.

"Don't be ridiculous. I was admiring the, um–"

I frantically search for anything of interest and merely say in a small voice, "Wood Panelling. It's an amazing design of, um, wood, and polish, rather traditional, wouldn't you say?"

Angie makes a face behind Luke's and I pray to God the cameras never picked that up.

"Thanks." I reach out and grab a glass of wine and he nods to the side.

"May I have a word?"

"Sure."

The curious glances sear into my back as I turn away and head to the side where a huge arrangement of poinsettias obscures us from the gawping crowds.

"Hey." Luke says in that sexy voice that should be illegal.

"Hey." I shift on my frozen feet and note that we wouldn't get anywhere near the fire that's roaring nearby, due to the number of villagers crowding around it.

'"Nice singing."

He raises his eyes and I giggle and then choke on the wine that almost hits him square in the face.

"I'm sorry."

I wipe my mouth with my glove and wish I was more like Morgana, with her elegance and poise. I'm a disgrace and really should have stayed at home.

"You've been avoiding me."

"No I haven't."

I try not to look at him but he shifts and blocks my view and whispers, "Why didn't you ask for me when you dropped the plan off this morning?"

"I didn't want to disturb you." I lie because I took the coward's way out.

He messaged me last night and asked me to drop it by this morning, or at least the bit I've done because he was meeting with his bank today and wanted something to show them. Morgana was here when I arrived and was so kind it struck me how much of a bitch I've become around him because all I can think of is I wish it was me with him instead of her. I was trying to remove the temptation.

He shakes his head. "Morgana told me you had to run."

"I did. I meant run errands, get to the post office, you know the kind of last-minute things us girls need to do."

I'm rambling because those chocolate eyes are sparkling in my direction, causing me to melt inside, my earlier deep freeze instantly thawed with one look from his soulful eyes.

"I don't suppose you'd meet me after this finishes?"

"Why?" I am genuinely confused and as Jasper appears like the genie from the lamp to spirit him away, Luke says over his shoulder, "Please, Jessy, it's, um, business."

My heart sinks as I watch him go because of course it is. It can *only* be business, which is why I am trying my best to stay away because breaking my heart this Christmas wasn't on my list to Santa.

CHAPTER 39
LUKE

I just can't catch a break.

All I want is a moment alone with Jessy, but fate is conspiring against me. As I hand out mulled wine while Morgana follows with mince pies, I'm reminded what a charade my life is. This whole scene is staged, much like my life, and it doesn't sit well with me exploiting good people to do the devil's work.

I fully consider reality TV the devil's work because if there is any actual 'real' at all in the title, it's the fact the 'real' is misspelled and meant to be 'reel'. It reels in the viewers to believe other people actually live like this. That they have the perfect lives, making the viewers' ones appear dull in comparison without realising the whole thing is staged.

Morgana laughs at something the villager is saying and yet despite my mood, I raise a smile. I love her so much, but more as a sister than anything. It was easy to agree to further her career while protecting mine, but now I want one person to know the truth and my fake life is stopping me from doing that.

An interminable age passes before the villagers decide to head home and leave us to clear up and for once I'm thankful for the production crew who take everything in their stride. Since they arrived, they have worked tirelessly to transform Granthaven Manor and its grounds into a scene from a Christmas movie.

They even deposited fake snow near the lake where I have shot endless scenes with Morgana as we walk hand in hand around it, stealing kisses and expressing how much we already love the place to the cameras thrust in our faces at all times.

We are recreating the magic of Christmas and weaving an impossible dream. I have no doubt this show will be a success because of all the ingredients set in place. Perfection comes at a price many can't afford to pay and must settle for watching other people live the dream instead.

But are they? I'm still to be convinced of that.

I keep my eyes sharpened on Jessy because if she tries to slip away, I will prove why I am paid so much and sprint after her, my training having reaped huge rewards as I attempt to get back in shape while sifting through my problems.

As soon as her family make to leave, I head over and say casually, "Jessy, I'm sorry to ask, but I could use a word about the business plan."

"What now?" her mother raises her eyes. "But it's nine o'clock – at night." She exclaims and her father says in a deep voice, "Prosperity never sleeps, Portia. That's why men like Luke are successful."

Portia nods, seemingly accepting his explanation, and turns to me.

"Well, if you could make sure she gets home, okay. I expect Wilf will be out searching for his Christmas dinner and I don't want that to be my daughter."

"His Christmas dinner?"

I'm confused and Jessy laughs softly. "Anything that moves, flies, or walks. Rabbits mainly, but they are probably safely tucked up in their burrows. I doubt he will be successful anyway and will resort to his neighbour dropping off turkey with all the trimmings on Christmas day instead."

"That's kind of her."

Portia smiles. "It's what we do, Luke. We care for our own and make sure everyone is okay and not on their own, especially at Christmas. Wilf prefers his own company but is still one of us and an extra meal is not a lot to give, but he appreciates the kindness."

"It's a special place." I concede as I look around me and register the happy laughter of the villagers as they head off into the night sky, their phones lighting their way once they return the lanterns to the crew.

I don't believe I have even met my neighbours in Cheshire. I think Morgana has, but I keep away from any social interaction if I can help it, preferring instead to train and spend time with the team rather than anyone not connected to football.

I love how Jessy's parents hug her tightly before they leave, issuing instructions not to be long and to make sure the door is locked behind her when she returns and I picture my parents far away in Florida, not even calling to check I'm okay.

They have always been like that, accepting that my life is football and from an early age I was sent to live with another family close to the academy while they carried on travelling without the burden of looking after me.

Morgana and Steven are my family now, and even that is a contrived one. We love one another but lie to protect our own interests and I am not prepared to do that anymore.

I want to start again.

To discover who Luke Adams really is and to share my life with somebody who loves me and not for what I can give them. Team Adams if you like. Two people who love one another and work together to make life meaningful. To raise a family and cultivate the next generation with love and kindness and a whole lot of fun.

As Jessy watches her parents leave, I picture her as the woman of my dreams, by my side forever. It feels good, right even, and strengthens my resolve. It's time to put my needs first for once and go and get my girl.

The commotion inside the manor reminds me we aren't alone, and I turn to Jessy and sigh heavily.

"We should head somewhere quieter."

"Okay?"

I can tell she's nervous and I suppose it was a strange request, but I couldn't let another night pass by without coming clean to Jessy and telling her exactly what's on my mind.

∼

We head to the room I've been using to train in. It's the one nearest the swimming pool, if you could call it that. I wouldn't actually jump in that water if I was on fire because it's unheated and has a green tinge to it. It's just another thing that requires money thrown at it and I am still undecided if it will be *my* money that saves this place. I have a perfectly good swimming pool at home in my mansion, heated to the perfect temperature, with comfy loungers set around it. I don't need another one, although technically I already do because back at home I enjoy the luxury of an indoor and an outdoor pool.

"I hope the evening was a success." Jessy says with laughter in her voice and I resist the urge to hold her hand as we head towards the other end of the house.

"It will be." I assure her. "Jasper will dub over the frankly excruciating singing and when you watch it back, it will resemble the scene from a movie. There will be no wailing and notes out of tune, just smiling faces enjoying the magic of Christmas."

"That's sad." She shakes her head.

"Why? Isn't that what everyone wants to see?"

"Not really." She shrugs. "People love to see failure. They laugh at the things that don't go according to plan because it's real. Social media is awash with people staging things that go wrong because it raises a laugh and gets the most views. If anything, it makes people feel better about their lives by reminding them that everyone makes mistakes. It's an acceptable form of madness and far more entertaining than watching someone getting everything right."

She laughs softly. "What is perfection, Luke? It's kind of boring, don't you agree?"

"I do."

We reach the makeshift gym and her eyes widen when she sees the room I spend most of my day in.

"Why here?"

"Because it's private and my personal space away from the madness. The only other place in this house is my bedroom, and I'm sure you agree that wouldn't be appropriate."

Her face blushes red and I groan inside because being around Jessy is the sweetest form of torture. When you want something you can't have so badly, it becomes the most important thing in your life and I want Jessy Potter more than I want to return to the game. She has *become* the game and I intend on winning and so I nod towards one of the bench presses.

"Sit with me, Jessy."

She appears nervous and I say with determination.

"There is something you should know."

As she sits gingerly beside me, I can tell she's nervous and for some reason so am I. I'm not sure how she will react to what I'm about to say and if I'm honest, I probably shouldn't be about to open Pandora's box, anyway.

CHAPTER 40
JESSY

I am so nervous. It's as if the air in this room is supercharged with destiny and I'm fearful of what that means for me and Granthaven.

I'm guessing Luke is about to tell me he's giving up. It's all too difficult and he will be heading home now his ankle is healed. I'm not stupid and realise it's probably for the best. Morgana won't want to live here. I doubt he does too because they take Granthaven on face value and haven't experienced the magic of the place.

Luke inhales and then exhales sharply, his fingers clenched in his lap, revealing he's anxious and my heart sinks as I whisper, "It's okay, Luke. It really is."

"What's okay?"

"Your decision." My voice catches as I whisper, "You're leaving, aren't you?"

"Leaving!" He shifts, so he is sitting astride the bench, effectively staring into my eyes and I flinch as he reaches out and turns my face to his and I note those damn eyes melting any barriers I have clumsily tried to erect against him.

"Of course I'm leaving, Jessy."

My heart sinks.

"I was always going to leave because my career is in Manchester."

"I see."

I lower my eyes and his soft husky voice wafts around my soul as he whispers, "But I'm coming back?"

"For one year, as in the terms of the will." I nod my understanding. "It's okay, Luke, you don't have to explain."

"I do, Jessy, because, well, that wasn't why I asked you to wait behind."

"Then why?" I'm curious and his eyes burn into mine as he says in a low voice, "I have a confession to make."

"A confession?"

He nods. "Morgana."

Oh holy hell, he's about to ask my opinion on how best to propose, or ask me to buy her a meaningful gift for him to place under the tree. That's what this is.

"What about her?"

My throat is dry and I wish there was a mulled wine lurking when I needed it, or some of that brandy would be good right now.

"She's not really my girlfriend."

His words float around my mind like strangers gate-crashing the party because they don't belong here. It takes me a moment to register what they mean, and I stare at him in surprise, noting the twinkle in his eye as he watches me.

"I don't understand."

The night the mistletoe died

I'm so confused, and he shocks me by lifting my hand and holding it gently in his and whispering, "Morgana's real name is Anna Morgan. She was a model who met Steven at a function he attended and they started dating."

"Steven!"

It's as if the mist is clearing because things are making a lot more sense now.

"Morgana wasn't born, but Anna was interested in pursuing the life of an influencer. She wanted to be with Steven and it presented her with the perfect opportunity to build her brand."

"But why pretend to be your girlfriend? I still don't understand that part."

"Because I was struggling to fend off the women who wanted their shot with me and to exploit it for money and fame."

"It must have been tough. You have my sympathy."

I roll my eyes and add, "It must have been soul destroying being the object of unwanted desire."

He laughs and his eyes twinkle, causing me to shift awkwardly on the bench. This is so unfair. He is just too attractive for his own good and my own sanity.

"So, Steven came up with the whole fake relationship thing. It kept the women away from me and gave Morgana the perfect platform on which to build her empire."

"It does kind of make sense."

I must agree and he whispers, "But I don't want to pretend anymore."

I'm in shock as his meaning is clear. He has fallen in love with his best friend's girl and is going to ask for my advice.

There can be no other reason why he asked me here, away from the crowds, so we can work out a way to remove Steven from the picture and get him the girl.

"I see."

I attempt to act concerned, as if I understand and, of course, he can ask me anything. It's what friends are for, after all. Mind you, if being a good friend is stealing your best one's girlfriend, I'm better off alone.

"You want my help?" I ask, and he raises his eyes.

"Your help?"

"In splitting them up so you can call her your girlfriend for real."

"NO!" He stares at me in shock. "Of course not."

"Phew, that's a relief."

I laugh with embarrassment and then shrug. "So, what do you want, Luke?"

"You, actually."

It's as if the world stops spinning and takes a quick break because nothing makes sense anymore. I must have entered a parallel universe and am now somebody else entirely, and I stare at him with confusion.

"For what?"

He says awkwardly, "For, um–"

Before he can finish his sentence, the door crashes open and Steven rushes in, holding up his hands and saying quickly, "Luke, you've got to call the club. It's urgent."

"Why?"

He appears agitated and I don't blame him because the expression on Steven's face isn't good.

"But–" He stares at me with a hopeless expression and I stand, shrugging off whatever this was and say with determination, "Take the call, Luke. We can talk tomorrow."

"But–" He stands as Steven points to the open doorway.

"They've been trying to reach you and they want a conference call with both of us. It sounds important."

Luke huffs with frustration and says apologetically. "I'm sorry, Jessy. Maybe give me a moment and I'll walk you home."

"Just go, Luke."

Steven heads out of the door and with a frustrated sigh, Luke follows him, leaving me a lonely figure watching them go, wondering why fate is so cruel sometimes.

I sit back on the bench and think about the past few minutes. I understood the look in his eye. He is interested in me and it was as if all the confusion disappeared and life took on new meaning.

Now he's been summoned back to real life, and it throws up one huge problem. If Luke and Morgana split up – in the eyes of the world, I could be the one held responsible. Luke will struggle between the two worlds and Granthaven will become a huge burden that also comes with emotional baggage.

When you are faced with getting everything you wanted, and a man stares into your eyes and trusts you with a secret that not many people know about, it means a lot.

My first thought is one of euphoria. Luke is interested in me. Jessy Potter. I'm not dreaming that. It was in his eyes and yet my heart is heavy because I accept it will only end in heartbreak for me.

I stand and walk slowly to the door, my head spinning with what I've learned. Could it work between us? The famous footballer and the graduate who knows nothing of real life?

Deep in my heart, I don't believe it can and if I am going to stand any chance of recovering from the after effects of that, I should shut this down before it's even begun.

CHAPTER 41
LUKE

I'm nervous. The expression in Steven's eyes tells me he's nervous, too. I'm also frustrated because once again my current life has edged aside the life I want for myself.

The one with Jessy in it.

The chance I have at being with a girl who makes me feel like a kid again lusting after his first crush. When she smiles, my heart beats faster and when she isn't in my sight, I'm searching for her. I love the way she speaks, the fire in her eyes when she doesn't agree with what I say and the fierce passion she holds for Granthaven and the people who live here.

She is also sweet, funny and good company and did I say intelligent? She is also the prettiest girl I have ever met with a natural beauty, unlike many of the girls who throw themselves in my path.

She is the woman I want to hold. To announce to the world she is mine and we are dating. I would be proud to walk beside her and share my life with her, but once again fate has intervened and I hope more than anything that she's still here when I've made that call.

Steven sits opposite me and I take my seat at the dusty desk, my nerves on edge because something in his expression tells me he's worried.

As I make the call, my fingers shake as I hold the phone and it reinforces how much I love what I do and it's only when I face the possibility of losing everything I've worked for that it truly registers.

I am a footballer.

It is who I am. It defines me and if I'm not a footballer anymore, I lose the biggest part of my soul.

"Luke."

The manager's voice is serious and my heart is beating extra fast as he says wearily, "How are things?"

"You tell me, boss." I take a deep breath. "What's this all about?"

"Ah, yes." He exhales sharply and I picture his deep frown, the lines on his weathered face etched in worry which is a permanent thing because the management of the club takes the brunt of the board's displeasure if things don't go their way.

"We've had a bid for you in the transfer window."

"I see."

My heart-rate increases as he sighs. "It's huge. Too huge to disregard, especially with you out of action."

"But I'm good, fighting fit."

Steven nods, listening to every word on speaker and the boss groans. "Listen, Luke, this is the last conversation I want to be having, especially with my star forward, but the club is a business and money talks."

"So, you're selling me."

My ears ring with a steady hum as I consider my life changing on the end of this call and he growls, "We are putting the offer to you and it's your decision."

"What offer?"

I hold my breath as he says gruffly, "Real Madrid has offered seventy-five million and a salary of fifteen million a year for you."

Steven stares at me in shock and I almost drop the phone as I freeze, his words completely unbelievable to me.

"Sponsorship deals and appearances will significantly boost that sum, and I strongly encourage you to seriously consider this offer."

It's as if I've hit the jackpot and never knew I had a ticket. This sum of money is life-changing for both me and Steven, who, as my agent, commands a hefty percentage of any deal we make.

"They want you in Spain by the end of January."

He sighs heavily. "Listen. This is a once in a lifetime offer, so you should consider it carefully. It may not be what you hoped for. A different country isn't for everyone, but this will set you up for life. The club doesn't want to lose you, but the money will buy us out of a hole."

He pauses for a moment and my mind races to keep up and then he says in a softer voice, "I know you'll do the right thing. Just tell me your decision as soon as possible. I've bought you a few days, but they want to start the legalities as soon as possible."

"Yes, um, of course. I'll um, let you know."

"Take care, son, speak soon."

The manager cuts the call, leaving me staring at a

shocked agent who has just scored a life-changing pay day for himself.

"What are you thinking?" He asks carefully, leaning forward and gazing at me with concern.

"That I have no choice." I shake my head. "I can't turn that kind of money down because it's not only me it affects."

Steven says with concern, "Take the couple of days the boss has given you to think it through, Luke. The decision is yours and nobody else's. It's a lot to think about, namely selling up and moving to Spain. It could be a long stay or a short one, but it is a stay all the same."

He nods towards the brandy bottle left over from Geoffrey Knight's visit.

"You look as if you need that."

"Sure, we can celebrate or drown our sorrows. Either is good for me right now."

As he pours the shots, I remember Jessy waiting and my heart races when I picture what that money could mean for her and Granthaven. It's a long-shot because I'm not even sure if she's interested, but it could be the saving of Granthaven and the making of me.

∼

IT DOESN'T TAKE LONG to down the shot of brandy and leave Steven to get over the shock and head off to meet up with Jessy.

As I walk, the production crew smile their greetings as they work on the next scene of their production. Tomorrow we are filming the pantomime and despite very few rehearsals, Jasper is keen to get it in the bag. I'm aware we don't have much longer before Christmas, and I'm also aware that Morgana intends to celebrate it back in Manchester with her family and friends.

Usually, I celebrate with them and host it in my mansion but this year it may all change because I can't think of a better place to celebrate Christmas than here at Granthaven Manor with the woman who may change my life if she'll have me.

When I head inside the room I left her in, my heart drops when I notice it's empty and the truth hits me.

I don't need to go and look for her. It's obvious she's not interested.

I've scared her off.

I laid it on too thick and she did the right thing and left before I could make a fool of myself even further. It appears that on the night all my dreams should have come true, I woke up before the most important part of it was played out.

CHAPTER 42
JESSY

I walked away.

Despite Luke's request to stay, I made a decision that will probably turn out for the best – for both of us. Luke doesn't need another problem in his life. He is not in the right frame of mind to start something before he's even ended his current situation. By the sounds of it, something important has come up and I doubt it involves this village or this house.

His old life – his current life is calling and rather than lose him just as I've found him, I'm walking away to preserve my sanity.

As expected, the air is frosty and the stars twinkle in the deep ebony sky, casting soft shadows across the lake that is bathed in a mist that will freeze in the morning. The snowflakes left at the switch of a button and there is no excited chatter in the air as the villagers anticipate a different kind of Christmas this year.

The air is still and not even a bird is awake to disturb

the peace and it's as if nature is hiding along with me and it's the safest place to be.

I make my way up the path and note the lamp on in the hallway. I head into the warm kitchen where the embers in the fire glow with the last traces of oxygen and I turn my attention to the kettle and make myself a mug of tea.

That's what we do in Granthaven. When big decisions are made, we make tea to help us. When we are lost or grieving, tea is the cure for all evils and when we entertain, the first thing we offer is a nice cup of tea.

I need it now because my heart is heavy and I'm aware I may have made the worst decision of my life. It was certainly the hardest because opportunities, hell – men like Luke, don't come into my life often, if at all.

I walked away from possibly the most amazing thing to have ever happened to me because I'm scared. I am already preparing myself for him to leave me before we even begin.

That is no basis for a relationship. A one-sided one with no choices. I am better off settling down with a man like me. Normal, I suppose, and not in a world of celebrity that I understand nothing about and frankly terrifies me.

I sit at the wooden table and stare into the dying fire. My hands wrapped around the mug, contemplating my decision.

I am a fool. I already realise that, but being with Luke in any capacity terrifies my soul.

~

MORNING ARRIVES and my heavy heart reminds me of what I did last night and I wonder what Luke thought when he set off to find me. He will realise I'm not interested and that's the saddest part of all. I *am* interested and more than is good for my health.

"Hey love, do you fancy a bacon sandwich?" Mum asks as I hover in the doorway, brushing the sleep from my eyes.

"Sure."

She nods towards the teapot on the table. "Help yourself. The tea is fresh. Your dad's chopping some logs. We are running out fast. Thank God the delivery is due later today."

As I help myself, mum says sharply, "Okay, tell me what happened?"

"Nothing happened." I lie, and she shakes her head and groans.

"I'm your mother. I know when something's happened and your face doesn't lie, love. You look as if you hardly slept a wink last night. Are you worried about the pantomime today?"

"Yes."

I seize on that to get her off my back, and her voice is firm as she flips the bacon in the frying pan.

"You'll be fine. It's not as if you don't know the bloody play. It's been the same one for the past thirty years, even before you were born. Even I could recite all the words. In fact, it's difficult to forget them no matter how hard I try."

I laugh softly and sip the sweet, calming tea.

"Is it the filming?"

"Yes." I lie and she huffs, "Pretend they aren't there. Just go through the motions and let the rest of the team worry about how it looks. Honestly, Jessy, there is absolutely nothing to worry about."

She turns back to her task and I ask carefully, "Mum–"

"Yes love."

"Have you ever regretted a decision and wished you'd made a different one?"

"Lots of times." She chuckles as she dishes the bacon onto the bread.

"Actually, I was offered a job as cabin crew once, with the national carrier, no less."

"You never said."

"It was not long after I met your father."

She drops the plate in front of me and smiles. "It was long haul. I would be away for most of the time and I was so besotted with him I hated that thought, so I turned it down and went to work at the local bank instead."

"And you regret that?"

"Of course. You see, if I had known then what I learned very quickly, I could have had it all."

"In what way?"

"Well–" She grabs her own sandwich and sits at the table and stares at me with a thoughtful gleam in her eye.

"If it's meant to be, it will work out regardless of the obstacles in the way. Your father would still be here on my days off and could have travelled with me on occasions. I would have seen the world and been paid for it with no regrets. You see–" She fixes me with her sharp gaze and says softly, "You owe it to yourself to seize every opportunity life throws at you because you only get one life and have no way of knowing what will work unless you try? Never give up your dream to suit someone else,

Jessy, because they may not be the person who progresses through life with you. Only you will make that journey and you owe it to yourself to live life to the full."

She takes a bite of her sandwich and I must ask, "So you wish you had travelled, but what if Dad found someone else?"

"Then he wasn't my destiny. You see, true love will survive even the most temporary of tests and that is all life is, Jessy. Several chapters all involving different things and you are lucky if that special person features in every one of them."

Dad heads inside, stamping the ice from his boots and blows on his frozen hands.

"Is there one of those for me?" He asks and mum rolls her eyes.

"Of course, pour yourself a cup of tea and I'll make you one as soon as I've finished mine."

As dad sits down, he smiles at mum and I note the tender moment they share and it strikes me that even after all these years, they are as deeply in love as they were at the beginning and it gives me hope that one day I will be as lucky.

CHAPTER 43
LUKE

I am still shocked when I wake in the morning. Last night was a lot. Too much, and when Jessy left, I had no reason to stay. I went to bed. I locked everyone out and retired to my room, but I didn't sleep. Not until the early hours anyway, because so much was racing through my mind.

Granthaven, the inheritance, Jessy, Morgana, Steven and the transfer. My ankle throbs along with my heart because it's as if the world is closing in on me.

I wanted to talk things through with Jessy. I had so much to say. I value her opinion as a person and when I found the room was empty, it resembled my heart.

I am alone.

I always have been really because the Luke Adams the public sees is a different man to me.

That is the part of the job I could do without, but I'm aware it's also a necessary part of the job because the sponsors demand that I maintain a high profile. Successful on and off the pitch and now I'm also the master of all I survey. This is a fantastic story worthy of movie deals, books and hours of content for whatever medium people prefer.

The there's Real Madrid. The pinnacle of many footballer's careers. The promised land, the golden goose if you like – the top of the pile and is an opportunity I would be a fool to pass by and my head is spinning with it all. But most of all, my heart is heavy because I gained so much in one night and then promptly lost the most important thing.

Today we are filming the pantomime which is being staged in the manor house for the first time in history. The usual venue is the village hall, but it's not big enough for the production crew and their equipment. Jasper is firing on all cylinders, and Morgana is in her element. I am looking forward to it for a different, more selfish reason.

I get to kiss Jessy.

This kiss will be all I have to show her how I feel. A declaration to the world if you like, although they won't realise the kiss is genuine, at least on my part.

It's all I can think about, which is sad really for a man many consider is beating women off with a stick. Morgana is my official girlfriend. How will it look when I kiss another while she watches?

"Luke!" The woman herself heads into the kitchen and smiles with excitement. "This is going to be so cool. I'm excited to see the manor house brought back to life as it was in the past. The crew are already doing an amazing job and it will be spectacular."

"I'm glad you're happy."

I nod to the seat beside me and she slips into it, reaching for the cafetiere and pouring herself a coffee.

"What's on your mind, hun?" She misses nothing, she never has, and sometimes I wished Morgana was my girlfriend for real. Not because I fancy her, or am jealous of Steven, but because of all the women I've ever met, she gets me. She is me in female form, which is why we get on so well, and she lowers her voice and whispers, "Things aren't working out with Jessy?"

"She walked away last night."

Her eyes widen as I sigh heavily. "I told her everything and then I was called away. I said I wanted to pursue things with her and when I returned from the call with the boss, she had gone."

"She was probably shocked – scared even."

Morgana's eyes cloud with worry. "It's a lot to take in when you're not of our world, Luke. Not everyone wants to be in the spotlight, and I'm guessing Jessy is one of them."

"So, what do I do?"

She shrugs. "Just don't give up. Tread carefully but keep on treading. Show her you are serious and try to meet her on her own terms."

"You're a wise woman, Morgana." I smile my appreciation, and she nods. "I'm not just a pretty face, you know."

"You don't have to tell me."

Jasper heads our way and groans. "The camera crew are having difficulties with their filters, or something along those lines and the props department needs more time, apparently, because the delivery of mistletoe hasn't arrived and is the main focus of the show."

"Can't we just go out and pick some?" I ask, wondering why it's such a drama, and Morgana sighs. "Honestly, Luke, do you ever listen?"

She shares an amused look with Jasper and says solemnly, "The whole subject of the play is that the mistletoe died when Lady Townsend passed away. It's a true story apparently because from that day on there has been no sighting of mistletoe in Granthaven at all. It's why we shipped it in."

"I never thought."

She cuts in, "You never do, Luke. Unless it involves a ball and a net you tune out of life."

Jasper nods and Morgana grabs her coffee mug and stands. "Come on, Jasper, let's go and check the items off the list so we know where we're at. Luke, we need you in make-up within the next thirty minutes. Don't be late. It's set up in the green bedroom overlooking the stables."

As they head off, I remember the legend and laugh to myself. As if that ever happened. There must be a bunch somewhere around, or it's not the right climate for it. Who cares anyway? It's only a parasite and is probably a good thing it's nowhere on my estate.

As the thought hits me, another one collides at the same time.

My estate.

Since when did I start thinking of it as *my* estate?

As I peer around the kitchen and take in the shabby decor and old-fashioned units, I picture my designer one back at my home in Cheshire and it hits me. I've found a home here that I never had there, and the idea of returning to Rangers or Real Madrid in Spain doesn't appeal to me at all because it would feel as if I'm betraying Jessy and Granthaven.

∼

I'M aware I have thirty minutes before I'm needed, and I head out to find Steven. As I walk, I keep my head down to avoid talking to anyone because this place is crowded with people and a lot to deal with.

I call him to locate him faster and he informs me he's in the study, checking over the contract and as I head inside, he peers up, a worried frown on his face.

"You've come to a decision, haven't you?"

"I have."

I head across to the bookcase and retrieve the almost empty brandy bottle and two glasses.

His eyes light with hope because my decision will have a profound effect on his bank balance and he must be anxious about that.

As I splash the brandy into the glasses, I say with a smile, "I know I'm making the right decision, so don't even attempt to talk me out of it."

As I hand him the glass, the frown lines have deepened, but it's as if a weight has shifted from my shoulders as I raise my glass and smile happily. "Make sure our passports are up to date and book the Spanish lessons because you and me my friend are heading to Madrid."

CHAPTER 44
JESSY

I'm so nervous for many reasons, but the main one is because Luke will be there and I'm not sure how he'll react because I walked out on him.

My heart is racing as I walk to the manor house with Angie, who is babbling with excitement as she goes over her lines.

"What if we're scouted? We might end up in Hollywood." She says with an eager grin.

"I doubt it." I shrug, although stranger things have happened.

I hate to bring her down because she is buzzing right now and she nods. "We will be an overnight sensation like the calendar girls. They will need us to go to Hollywood to discuss the feature film. Probably casting some top actress to play me."

"Only the best." I add and she nods, her eyes shining.

"I can imagine us at the premiere now. Or even better, attending the unveiling of our stars on the Hollywood Walk of Fame."

"Walk of shame, more like." I raise my eyes and she drops her gaze and mumbles, "It was only one night and well, we have been out on a few dates already."

Last night, Angie didn't come home and asked me to cover for her. When she left the carol service, she was picked up by a guy from work and they went clubbing in Weymouth. Luckily for her, Margery and Terry are late risers and she managed to sneak in before they discovered she never came back. I am now seriously concerned for my friend because Stefan is due to head back to Sweden in the New Year when his visa is up and Angie is seriously thinking of throwing in her training and heading there with him.

It's as if change is swirling around me like a virus, promising to infect everything and everyone that means something to me. Luke and Morgana will undoubtedly head back to Manchester and it seems that Angie will be heading off for a new life in Sweden, of all places. Meanwhile, I am so busy ignoring opportunity, I will be the one left behind to pick up the broken pieces of a village that never really made it to the century we live in now.

The conversation with my mum is haunting me, as I wonder if I made the wrong decision last night. It's not as if Luke asked me to marry him or anything. I completely overreacted. He only said he was interested. That interest could last an hour, a day, or a week, possibly months, even years and, who knows, possibly a lifetime.

I will never find out. I am the stupid one who was so scared she fled like Cinderella when the clock struck twelve. Now I must kiss the prince despite everything, and I'm not sure how I feel about that.

∼

ONCE AGAIN, we head into the manor house and witness a transformation that causes my breath to hitch.

"Wow!" Angie gasps and rightly so, as the place has been catapulted back in time and is the image of what it must have been like back then.

It's giving off period drama vibes and I stare in amazement at the grand tapestries and art on the walls, with swags of holly and berries and burning candles in arches on the mantlepiece. The huge tree in the hallway glitters like the brightest jewel and the chandelier that sparkles from the ceiling is surely a work of art.

The grand staircase is dressed with foliage and red ribbons, and the fire is roaring in the grate, dancing seductively in front of my eyes.

"This is fantastic." Angie gasps as Jasper prowls our way wearing a headset.

"Head to make-up and wardrobe in the green room upstairs, ladies. We don't have a minute to waste."

We do as he says with open mouths, taking in every detail of the transformation.

"How have they pulled this off?" Angie whispers but I can't answer her and gasp, "It's a miracle."

"It's called prop warehouse, actually."

A woman walks past us with another headset on. "We had it shipped down from London and it must all be back within a week or we pay more."

'She scurries past and I note even the paintings on the landing wall are fake masterpieces and I whisper in awe, "It's as if we have stepped back in time. This pantomime will never be beaten. I can't believe they have gone to so much trouble."

"But where is the mistletoe?" Angie appears horrified as she says in a worried voice, "It's the main theme of the show. Lady Townsend loved it and had huge bunches of it in every swag, every wreath, and every arrangement. I can't see any."

"It probably didn't get here in time."

I share her worry though because without mistletoe, the show has no meaning.

Another production member overhears us and adds, "Don't worry, we'll superimpose it afterwards. The end result will show it everywhere. It's the power of the digital age."

"That's, um, good." Angie smiles and when they leave, she raises her eyes. "They may as well superimpose all of us, too. I wouldn't put it past them."

It makes me giggle and as we head into the green bedroom, I am caught up immediately in costumes and make-up and there is no time to think about anything else.

∼

I AM SO nervous and not because of the pantomime. I catch sight of Luke across the room as we have our briefing, and he appears deep in thought. He hasn't looked at me once and my heart thumps inside me as I devour his gorgeous face, committing every inch of it to memory because I'm positive he will be leaving us soon.

Then he looks up and our eyes connect and I'm caught staring, causing a heated blush to stain my skin.

His soft smile puts me at ease and I return it, wishing like crazy I could rewind the clock back to when we were sitting on the bench. My answer would be very different now to what it was then because the moment I saw him, it hit me hard.

I don't want to lose the chance to know him.

To discover what we can be and to become friends more than anything else.

He raises his eyes and nods toward Jasper, pulling a face as he reels off instructions that nobody is listening to.

Then Morgana takes over and I tear my eyes from Luke's and gaze at the woman many of us only dream about being as glamorous.

"Guys, just forget about the crew, where you are and what's happening around you. Just concentrate on your words and act your parts as if you are alone in the room. It always works for me and even now when I do this for a living, I am that young girl in her bedroom with a hairbrush as a microphone pretending to be grown up. It never leaves you. Nothing ever really changes, just the venue and the people who are visiting your room. So, most of all, enjoy the experience and remember the day you were famous for a while and tell it to your kids and grandkids and know that you will make them proud."

Her eyes find mine and she flashes me a brilliant smile. "Jessy, you will make an amazing Lady Townsend. I have every faith in you and Luke–" She swings her gaze to his and whispers, "I have every faith in you, baby. I will always be your number one fan."

I catch my breath as the cameras follow every move

we make and Morgana raises her clip board in the air and yells, "Now break a leg everyone and let's make this the best pantomime Granthaven has ever presented."

CHAPTER 45
LUKE

Jessy looks amazing. The beautiful powder blue silk costume complements the blue in her eyes and the make-up she is wearing is absolutely perfect. She is wearing a costume wig that isn't dissimilar to her own light blonde hair, and I can't stop staring at her.

Everything is going well. The fact all the lines are on autocue takes the nerves away and the moment I have been waiting for comes sooner than I anticipated.

We are to walk down the staircase hand in hand to greet our guests who are congregated around the huge tree and as we wait at the top on the landing, Jessy's soft hand feels so fragile in my much larger one. I wonder why I feel so protective of her. It's as if I want to wrap her in my arms and hold on forever, reassuring her that I've got her and we are a team who can take on the world.

She is silent, wrapped in her own thoughts and I don't want to break the spell, but this is my one chance to make my case before the play tears us in opposite directions.

"Jessy." I whisper as we wait for our cue.

She turns and looks at me and I whisper, "I'm sorry about last night."

I detect a spark of disappointment in her eyes and I expect she hates to be reminded of what I said and I say quickly, "Please let me explain. I promise not to pressure you, but will you meet me later for a drink when this charade is over?"

"Where?"

She smiles, which gives me hope at least, and I whisper huskily, "I'll come and find you after the play."

"Okay."

She smiles shyly, and it's like a dart of happiness to my heart.

We hear our cue and as we descend the stairs, Jessy says loudly, *"Oh Barnaby, this is my favourite time of the year. Christmas is such a magical time, but mainly because I get to share it with you."*

"My darling, Marianne, nothing means more to me than you and without you, there would be no Christmas."

"Oh, Barnaby, you do say the nicest things."

I can tell Jessy is struggling not to laugh at the corny lines we are reciting and as we reach the bottom of the staircase, I glance up and pull her to a stop.

"I spy a sprig of mistletoe, my darling, it would be bad luck to–"

Before I can say another word we hear a loud, "I found some!"

"Cut!" Jasper yells and we all stare at Wilf, who is red-faced and panting as he rushes in through the door, his gun slung over one shoulder and a huge bunch of mistletoe in his other hand.

"Oh my God." Morgana cries as she rushes towards him and retrieves the mistletoe from his hand.

"Where did you find it?"

"In Pike's wood. I nearly missed it, but as I was walking, it fell from the sky in front of my feet."

He beams proudly. "A bird flew off and I expect it was carrying it and yet when I looked up there was one of the biggest bunches I have ever seen. I can't believe we missed it."

I stare at Jessy, who appears to be in shock, and Jasper says loudly, "String it up."

As a crew member races to hang it on an arrangement that we must pass under, Jessy turns to me and smiles shyly.

I grip her hand tightly and I can't tear my eyes from her and as the commotion dies down, we are unaware of the cameras at all.

I repeat my earlier words, *"I spy a sprig of mistletoe, my darling. It would be bad luck to pass under it without stealing a kiss."*

Her voice trembles as she says softly, *"I will never deny you a kiss, Barnaby. You have my heart and you always will."*

I run my hand around her slender waist and pull her gently towards me. Her breath hitches as she holds my gaze and I note the soft gleam in her eyes and the quiver to her soft red lips.

Her eyes sparkle as her chest rises and falls against the period costume and as I lower my face to hers, her sweet breath caresses my skin like a feather.

My eyes gleam as I tentatively touch my lips to hers and with my other hand, I gently cup her face and run my thumb against her delicate skin. It takes one second for our lips to touch and as I close my eyes, I am lost in the sensation of tasting Jessy's lips for the first time.

It's like a homecoming and as she shifts a little closer, she reaches up, her fingers brushing against my cheek and I deepen the kiss, in no hurry to stop, treasuring the moment when I finally get my wish.

It's as if nobody else is here and now I've started I can't stop and tug her closer. I never appreciated the power of a kiss before, and I don't want to stop. I *can't* stop and Jessy isn't complaining. In fact, she is kissing me back, both of us reluctant to pull away.

When we finally remember there are close to thirty people watching us, I rest my forehead against hers and whisper, *"Happy Christmas my darling."*

"Happy Christmas, Barnaby."

Her soft giggle causes me so much happiness I have to fight my desire to steal another kiss and as the cheering starts, I don't even register it's not part of the show. Taking her hand, I turn and nod to the gawping crowd of villagers, *"Happy Christmas, Granthaven. Now, let's celebrate in the traditional way."*

∽

THE SHOW MUST GO on and it does. We act out the rest of the scenes without a hitch and by the time the pantomime ends and Granthaven is left a village in mourning, Morgana steps forward and addresses the camera.

"This play is based on a true story and to this day, Mistletoe has never grown in the village. However, today that changed when it was found again, along with the new 'Lord' of Granthaven making this his home. Luke Adams inherited this estate and never knew what it involved. We came here not really appreciating the sense of community and the spirit that never died."

She turns and calls me forward and smiles lovingly. "Luke has fallen in love with Granthaven and I know will do right by the village, so, happy Christmas, Luke and happy Christmas, Granthaven. May the mistletoe flourish and love be restored to the village and everyone who lives here."

As I kiss Morgana on the cheek, she nestles against me and as our hands clasp together we are the perfect picture of love and happiness, and it's true. Morgana will always be incredibly important to me and always part of my family, but it's time for us both to pursue our dreams and close this chapter in our own story so we can begin the next one.

CHAPTER 46
JESSY

As the villagers drift back to their homes, I make my excuses to my parents and Angie and slip away to the gym, where I arranged to meet Luke.

The crew are tearing down the 'set' as they call it, and Jasper and Morgana are somewhere plotting the next part of their reality show, leaving me to wonder what Luke is about to say.

As I walk, my lips still burn from the kiss earlier. I lost myself for a moment as something shifted between us. It was almost as if we were alone in the room. We weren't acting anymore, at least I wasn't and as I lost myself in his kiss, for a moment I imagined things really could work out for us.

As I head inside the gym, my heart flutters when I see Luke sitting astride the bench, a bottle of champagne on the floor beside him, with two glasses.

"Are you celebrating something?" I ask, raising my eyes and he inclines his head. "I hope so."

I hover uncertainly beside the bench and he pats it and says softly, "Now, where were we?"

As I join him, it strikes me that I'm not self-conscious anymore. Perhaps it was the kiss or the way I am so comfortable around him.

He bends down and lifts the bottle in one hand and then one of the glasses and he pours some champagne into the glass and hands it to me before doing the same with the other one.

He says nothing until he touches his glass to mine and says in his sexy voice, "To new chapters."

"To new chapters." I add, "Not that I understand what it means, but I'm intrigued."

"I'll let you in on a secret." I note the light in his eyes and wonder what it could be and he whispers, "I had a call from the manager of the club yesterday."

I try not to let my nerves show as I wait for him to ruin my life.

"I'm being transferred in the new year, subject to a full medical, of course."

"Transferred?" I smile. "Please tell me you're moving to Arsenal. Life would be a lot easier for you around here."

"Sadly, no, but it is a life-changing opportunity."

My breath hitches because this doesn't sound good for me or for Granthaven.

"I'm heading to Spain. Madrid."

"That's—" I can't form words because my heart has just crashed and burned and from the excitement in his eyes, Luke is more than happy about it.

"It's a golden opportunity that I would be a fool to pass up. Very few footballers get the opportunity to play for one of the most successful clubs in the world. It will help so many people too; people who are close to me. I can't turn them down."

"So you can choose?" I'm not sure why I'm asking him that because it's obvious he's more than happy about it, and he nods. "I can turn it down, but I'd be a fool to do that."

I raise my glass. "Well, it's congratulations then. I'm happy for you, Luke. That's great news."

I paint a smile on my face while my heart is giving up. I knew this would happen and all the hope I had after we kissed has been crushed with his news.

"So–" He raises his glass and touches it against mine and says huskily, "It means I will have the money to make our plans a reality."

"Our plans?" I'm confused, and he nods with an excited gleam in his eye.

"Your business plan, Jessy. Renovating the houses, the barns and the manor house. Bringing new business to Granthaven to ensure its longevity."

"I'm sorry, Luke, but well, um, how? You will be living in Spain."

"Which is why I need a business manager. It's why I need you."

"I see."

I knew it was too good to be true. This is about business and not my heart.

I attempt to disguise my feelings and smile. "You will have to spell it out for me because I'm not really understanding what's going on right now."

He surprises me by taking the glass from my hand and setting them both down on the floor, he takes my hands in his and stares at me with a soft gleam in his eye.

"Morgana and Steven are returning to Cheshire in a few days' time. I am not."

My heart beats a little faster as he whispers huskily, "My heart is here, Jessy, with you and the village."

"You're staying?"

I can't hold back the huge grin on my face as he nods. "I know it's inappropriate because you're my employee and well, you may not want anything other than a professional relationship with me, but Jessy Potter – well – I don't suppose you're free tomorrow evening."

"I may be."

I'm suddenly rather shy as he winks. "Then would you like to go out, for dinner perhaps, on a kind of date?"

I note the anxiety in his eyes as he waits for my response and I squeeze his hands and whisper, "I thought you'd never ask."

"I have another question." He leans a little closer and, as his lips hover against mine, he whispers, "Do you have a passport?"

I don't even get to answer as his lips crash onto mine and this time our kiss is a lot deeper and holds more meaning because all of my doubts dissolve like the bubbles from the champagne as life gives me a second chance to live the dream – wherever it takes me.

EPILOGUE
JESSY

One month later

Tonight is bitter sweet because Luke heads off to Spain tomorrow to begin training. We are spending the evening at the manor house and we are not alone.

Morgana and Steven are here for the weekend. They are also affected by the move and Steven has been busy arranging it. Morgana is here in a different capacity, though, because she wants Luke's approval for the show they filmed at the manor.

We gathered in the sitting room to watch it and as the fire crackles in the grate I love that Luke's arm is slung around my shoulders as I nestle against him, loving how close we are already.

It's been a very busy month.

We've had endless meetings with Geoffrey Knight and the bank manager, planning the restoration of Granthaven based on Luke's income, along with that of the estate. Luke also appointed a solicitor to investigate setting up a trust that will protect Granthaven in the future, should anything happen to him. Luke wants to future proof the village so that one man alone doesn't own it outright.

He is setting up a trust. The Granthaven trust and hopefully all the income from the business will be ploughed back into it, to bring it into the modern age without compromising its heart.

We are at the early stages but have a plan at least and tomorrow Luke heads to Spain to begin the new chapter of his football career.

"It's on."

Morgana grips Steven's leg, and he groans. "I'm not blind."

Morgana grins. "I can't wait to see it."

Luke squeezes my shoulder and rolls his eyes. "I'm dreading it."

"Oh, Luke, you'll be fine. Don't be so silly." She says with a cheeky grin and as the music starts, we turn our attention to the screen.

I watch in awe as the story of Granthaven plays out on the screen. The familiar roads, landscape and people wrapping like a cosy blanket around me. It looks magical, beautiful even, and the power of the digital age has transformed it from being uncared for, into a spectacular piece of living history.

It's as if we are stepping back in time. Jasper has worked a miracle because he brought it back to life in the most creative of ways.

Morgana and Luke are the perfect stars of the show

and as I watch them together on the screen, I understand why they are so popular, or should I say *were*.

It was the story of Christmas, when Morgana announced they were separating, but would always remain the best of friends. They issued a joint statement where they revealed they had become more like friends than anything else, and with Luke's transfer to Spain, Morgana had decided to pursue her interests closer to home. It signified a natural break for them and they would continue as the best of friends in the future.

It seemed to work too because after the outpouring of grief from their fans, it's now business as usual as they carry on with their lives.

Morgana and Steven spent Christmas together in Cheshire and Luke spent it with us. We pulled together and made it a Christmas to remember, with Angie and her family joining mine at the manor house, where we all made Christmas special for Luke's first one in Granthaven.

It was a special time where we cooked, drank far too much and played games, before watching the Christmas television in front of the roaring fire.

Luke's gift to me was a meaningful one because when I opened the small box on Christmas day, the necklace I had admired in Dorchester was nestled between the tissue paper in the box.

"How did you know?"

I gasped, and he smiled and told me that Morgana went back and bought it.

I was so surprised because back then I thought they were together and Luke told me he had confessed how much he liked me soon after he first met me. I felt like a fool because I had so nearly passed up on love because I never really thought I was good enough for him. However, he has cast all those doubts aside, and I truly believe I can cope with anything life throws at us.

I snuggle in closer and when the part where the pantomime comes on, I stare riveted at the screen as the familiar scenes are played out before me.

"Wow, it almost looks professional." I say wryly and Morgana says proudly, "Jasper edited in lots of details and also took out anything that wasn't so good."

"Like the carol singing."

It was hilarious when that part came on because Jasper had dubbed a choir over our voices, cutting out the dreadful singing and replacing it with perfection. Even Wilf's gun was airbrushed out and yet I much prefer the reality than the dream.

It's what I love about life here. The fact nothing is perfect, which in its own way makes it even more perfect in my eyes. Perfection isn't something that has no rough edges or flaws because they are what tells the story. They are what builds meaning and makes for an interesting tale.

Where is the interest in something that hasn't had a few knocks to celebrate the triumphs as well as commiserate on the failures? That is life, with all its good points and bad ones. That is what makes life interesting, not one where nothing goes wrong and everything appears perfect. It's more relatable to witness the flaws in others because that is what makes us human after all.

As the credits roll and the story is left with a happy ending, the camera pans to a shot of a bunch of mistletoe hanging in the tree. Yes, love was restored to Granthaven

Manor, and the fortunes changed of everyone who lived in the village because of one kiss under the mistletoe on a very special Christmas Eve.

∼

If you liked this story, you may want to check out my other Christmas books.

Thank you for reading The Night The Mistletoe Died. If you liked it, I would love if you could leave me a <u>review</u> as I must do all my own advertising.

This is the best way to encourage new readers and I appreciate every review I can get. Please also recommend it to your friends as word of mouth is the best form of advertising. It won't take longer than two minutes of your time, as you only need write one sentence if you want to. Please note this book is written in UK English which can differ from the US version.

Have you checked out my website? Subscribe to keep updated with any offers or new releases.

sjcrabb.com

When you visit my website, you may be surprised because I don't just write Romantic comedy.

I also write under the pen name M J Hardy. I send out a monthly newsletter with details of all my releases and any special offers but aside from that, you don't hear from me very often.

If you like social media, please follow me on mine where I am a lot more active and will always answer you if you reach out to me.

Why not take a look and see for yourself and read Lily's Lockdown, a little scene I wrote to remember the madness when the world stopped and took a deep breath?

Lily's Lockdown

ALSO BY S J CRABB

Christmas Books

My Christmas Billionaire

Christmas in Dream Valley

My Christmas Romance

Holly Island

A Special Kind of Advent

My Christmas Boyfriend

Dream Valley

Cruising in Love

Coming Home to Dream Valley

New Beginnings in Dream Valley

Christmas in Dream Valley

Standalone

The Diary of Madison Brown

My Perfect Life at Cornish Cottage

Jetsetters

More from Life

Fooling in love

Will You

Escape to Happy Ever After

Aunt Daisy's Letter

Sequel

The Wedding at the Castle of Dreams

sjcrabb.com

Printed in Great Britain
by Amazon